Out of Time

a collection of short stories

by

MARIA SAVVA

Published by:
Rose and Freedom Books
P.O. Box 55285
London N22 9EU
England, U.K.

Cover photo by Koan at Morguefile.com

A catalogue record of this book is available from the British Library

ISBN: 978-0-9928345-5-5

The Stories

1. The Ring
2. Gunshot
3. Change of Heart
4. In the Past
5. Family Ties
6. The Games People Play
7. Where Do We Go?
8. One Chance
9. lex talionis
10. Think Twice
11. Ain't That Peculiar?

Bonus Stories - (from the Mind's Eye series)

1. Love and War
2. Blowin' in the Wind
3. Oblivion
4. Repercussions
5. On the Rocks
6. Secrets of the Forest
7. Shadows
8. Escape
9. The Great Flood
10. Glimmer Siluridae
11. Lost in You
12. The Memory Remains
13. The Chocolate Fiend
14. The Great Painter
15. Somewhere In Time
16. Sand and Water

Acknowledgements

The original versions of the first eight stories in this collection were published on *The Write Launch* (thewritelaunch.com) - an online literary magazine - in 2017. Thank you to Sandra Fluck, and the team, for believing in my writing and the stories, and for publishing them on your site.

Thank you to Bob Helle, for the valuable editing advice.

Thank you to Darcia Helle, for inviting me to submit a short story for your newsletter anthology and short story collection. Your request motivated me to write three new stories, "lex talionis", "Think Twice", and "Ain't that Peculiar". Thanks for your editing advice on "lex talionis", and for publishing the original version of that story in your anthology.

Thank you to Julie Elizabeth Aldridge, Michael Radcliffe, Kim Stapf, Helle Gade, Maria Haskins, Neil Schiller, and Martin David Porter.

For Evita, Brenna, Tadhg, Niamh, and Ernest.

The Ring

Paige pulled her coat closer, battling against the chill wind. Autumn consistently brought its own coldness to Paige's mind, something that could not be so easily deflected. The memories lived deep inside her psyche and ventured out when the days became shorter, bringing shadows from the past with them—not that they were ever really dormant for long. Remnants and reminders remained, sticking fast like a stubborn stain despite the tides of life and time.

I was only a child, was the mantra she relied on to drown out the accusatory inner voices whenever they disturbed her peace. The words had a soothing effect; *I was only a child.* But the blaming voices always returned.

There remained a sense of nostalgia mixed with grief whenever she remembered her college days. All the happy memories were tarnished by this one regret and, consequently, only accessible after bypassing a mire of trauma, debris, and destruction.

Somehow Paige managed to hide her torment from friends and family, maintaining a calm exterior. She'd married quite young and was the mother of two well-adjusted children: George, ten, and Mia, sixteen. There were five months to go until Mia's seventeenth birthday, then the child would be the same age as Paige had been when life had changed forever. As Mia's birthday drew closer, the tension grew stronger so that most mornings Paige woke up, after a restless night, feeling suffocated by the weight of what she'd done and the repercussions.

∽∾

Paige hopped onto the bus, having made the decision today—on the eve of her fiftieth birthday—to finally face the fear and guilt. The time had come. Peace of mind would remain a distant dream until the darkness that lingered was confronted and banished.

The journey seemed to take an eternity, but eventually the bus pulled up to the kerb. It had been a while since she last visited this place but not much had changed.

Negotiating the busy high street, Paige attempted to block out the negative voice in her head saying this was too little too late. At the entrance to the alleyway, which led to the back of the college, long forgotten recollections flared up causing a mixture of emotions ranging from mirth to gloom. She walked an obstacle course of echoes from the past.

The oak tree came into view: a long lost friend; the keeper of secrets for so many years. The place appeared untouched, as if frozen in time waiting for this day.

It's been here all along. Why did you wait so long? You could have come here years ago. You could have made everything okay. You always were a coward. Why didn't you tell her sooner? Why didn't you tell him? It was only a bus ride away. All these years you've wondered. You're so stupid. Silly girl. You messed up their lives. Did you actually think it would make a difference? Jealousy, that's what it was, you know. You're such a loser. Why are you here now? What difference will it make after all these years?

She shook away the derisive thoughts.

A leaf fell from the tree, landing above the mound where the ring was buried. Surveying the surroundings to make sure there were no witnesses, Paige took the trowel from her handbag and began to dig, uncovering, breaking through, shaking off the soil, digging deep. With each layer, a little more of the ever-present anxiety was whittled away. *I'll find the ring, soon, and return it—then I can relax, at last.* Even as those hopeful thoughts attempted to ease her mind, she knew it wouldn't be that simple to forget. This secret had endured for over thirty years, had become a part of her, had shaped her. Letting go would be akin to separating from a long-term partner. The habitual, no matter how warped, invariably feels more comfortable.

ᴨᴥᴧ

Ava had shown the ring to Paige in the morning on their way to college: a beautiful gold ring set with one perfect diamond, with a twist of delicate white gold encircling the jewel. It gleamed more radiantly than any piece of jewellery Paige had ever seen. She blinked, hoping it would disappear, hoping it might just be a dream. On opening her eyes, however, Ava's brilliant smile shone brightly. Paige watched on as her friend snapped shut the ring box and placed it carefully in her bag.

'I found it in the drawer, in his bedroom,' Ava explained, the soppy smile not showing any signs of waning. 'He's asked me to dinner tonight;

says he has something important to ask me. I wanted to show it to you, but I'm going to put it back later before we go out.'

Ava's ecstatic mood and giddy laughter was too much for Paige to bear.

James had been Paige's first love. They'd never actually been a couple but were best friends at school and did everything together. Paige simply assumed they'd end up married, unconsciously planning her future around that.

When they started college and met Ava, everything changed. Ava and James became a couple overnight, it seemed. With no period of adjustment to allow Paige to come to terms with the changes, it felt like a betrayal.

One day, James said, 'I'm going to the cinema with Ava tonight.' He appeared so happy and went on to say, 'I've never had a real girlfriend before: you're the only girl I've been friends with, but we're just mates. It feels weird, actually. Maybe I'm growing up!'

The sudden realisation that he didn't feel the same way came as a shock to Paige.

She imagined James proposing to Ava, placing the ring on her finger, and the couple's inevitable kiss. The reasoning behind stealing the ring was to delay James's proposal until she could figure out what to do. Burying the ring wasn't a carefully constructed plan, but more of a desperate act.

It proved easy enough to steal the ring from Ava's bag. Burying it beneath the oak tree was supposed to be a temporary solution. She almost went back to get it a couple of times, but when Ava and James broke up it just didn't seem as important. They left college a few months later, and Paige decided to leave the ring under the tree and to try to forget about it. Even after years passed by, however, the constant niggling guilt over having stolen the ring and changing the course of Ava and James's lives, proved a heavy burden to bear.

❧

As Paige continued to dig, the box came into view. Although covered in mud, it hadn't eroded. Eyes closed, Paige pulled out the box as if exhuming a dead thing. She shuddered at the realisation that it did represent death, in a way; the death of a blossoming romance. She'd purposefully driven a wedge between her two closest friends and contributed to the end of their relationship, and for what? Nothing had been gained except a lifetime of regret.

The tiny box brought to mind Ava's smiling face, a reminder of when she'd first shown the ring to Paige. Then an image of James entered her mind's eye as she recalled the time he'd revealed he was in love with Ava, a look of delight on his face.

Paige dared not open the box; it contained other people's thwarted dreams.

The painful memories assailed her... Ava's tears on confessing to Paige about losing the ring had eclipsed the smile she'd worn earlier when telling her about finding it in James's room... James blamed his mother for stealing the ring. Ironically, it had been Paige he'd offloaded to:

'My bloody mum took the ring. I was gonna propose to Ava, but now it's all ruined.'

'Are you sure your mum took—'

'Of course I'm sure. She's a thief. She's been taking things from me and my brother for years so she can sell them and pay off her gambling debts.'

Paige avoided his eyes. Couldn't bring herself to tell him the truth. 'I'm sorry, James,' was all she said.

'Sorry? It's not your fault. Oh, do you know what, maybe it's the universe sending me a sign, or something. I'm too young to settle down, ain't I?'

'Um...'

'That's what it is.'

James and Ava dated for a couple more months then parted. Ava broke down one day and admitted to James that she'd taken the ring and had then lost it. That had led to their separation, as far as Paige knew. She'd kept her distance from the couple so couldn't be sure.

Paige's own relationship with James became strained. They lost touch within months of leaving college.

Paige left the ring buried, despite knowing what James and Ava were going through. Over the years she'd questioned herself about it, again and again; why hadn't she dug up the ring and found a way to return it to James all those years ago? The answer never came.

಄಄಄

The reason Paige had come here to dig up the ring was so that she could

4

return it to James. She intended to post the ring to him. Anonymously. Standing here under the oak tree, the box in her hand, voices of doubt began to stir. *Does it even matter anymore? Why bother? The damage has been done. James might not even be living at the same address. If it does reach him, what will he think when it turns up in the post? He might be able to trace the parcel back to me.* Paranoia reared its head; a feeling she had grown accustomed to.

Paige stood staring at the ring box. How could it be possible that this small piece of jewellery, this inanimate object, had caused so much anxiety?

She placed the muddy trowel into a plastic bag before putting it back into her handbag, along with the ring box.

Paige held back tears and turned towards the high street. She walked swiftly, trying to avoid overthinking by looking in shop windows.

Stopping outside a jeweller's, a ring that was displayed as a centerpiece in the window caught her eye. It was identical to the one in her bag. There was no mistaking the design: the ring had haunted her dreams for many years, the image of it ingrained like a subconscious tattoo. Questions flooded her mind: *How did it get there? Did someone find it? But why would they have taken the ring and buried the box again?*

Just then, a woman's voice called out to her. The voice sounded strange but familiar at the same time.

'Paige? Paige, is that you?'

She saw a middle-aged woman emerge from the shop doorway. *Ava?* Paige put a hand to her mouth.

Ava approached, arms outstretched, and hugged Paige tightly. 'Wow! Long time no see. What are you doing here? Do you still live around here?'

'Um... no, I... I was just passing through.'

'Come in for a cup of tea. We must catch up! James is at home with the kids; shame, he would have loved to see you. You know, you've hardly changed; you look the same!'

'Did you say *James?*'

'Yes. James and I own this shop. Come inside and I'll tell you all about it.'

☙❧

'Oh, Paige. I can hardly believe you're here,' said Ava, setting a pot of tea on the table after pouring two cups.

Ava had introduced Paige as "one of my dearest old friends", to the staff in the jewellery shop before inviting her upstairs to the kitchen area.

'Isn't it funny how time flies? The last time we saw each other we were teenagers, now look at us!' said Ava as they sat opposite each other at the kitchen table.

Paige laughed. 'I'll be fifty tomorrow.'

'You don't look a day over twenty-one.' Ava giggled.

'Oh, maybe just a day.' Paige joined in with the laughter but felt awkward having this light-hearted conversation with Ava; she couldn't help wondering how welcoming Ava would have been if she'd known the truth.

'Fifty is the new thirty,' quipped Ava. 'Happy Birthday! Let's have a bit of cake to celebrate. I made a chocolate cake last night, actually.' Standing up, she busied herself taking plates out of the cupboard along with a cake tray.

Paige watched her. Ava hadn't changed much, was still as pretty as she used to be, with her delicate features and wavy blonde hair. Her hair was speckled with grey now but retained a beautiful glossy sheen. She'd hated Ava for being so pretty when they were teenagers, when James had fallen for her. Now, though, there was just an overwhelming sense of sadness that they'd lost touch for so many years.

'Fifty is a big birthday; are you having a party?' asked Ava.

'No. I don't celebrate my birthdays much these days.'

'I know what you mean, although James and I had a massive party this year for our joint fiftieths. It's quite a milestone if you think about it.'

'It is.'

'So, tell me all about what you've been doing all these years,' she said, placing a plate with a large slice of creamy chocolate cake in front of Paige.

'Thank you. It looks delicious.'

'Are you married? Kids? Career?'

'I have two children and have been married for twenty-three years. My husband, Michael, is a teacher at our local primary school.'

'I'd love to meet him, and your children.' Ava sighed. 'Why did we ever drift apart, hey? We should have kept in touch. You, me, and James, we were like the three amigos, weren't we?'

Paige forced a smile as so many memories erupted. None of this made sense. Had Ava married James after all?

'I suppose when I stupidly lost the engagement ring, things changed a bit, didn't they? I was such a fool back then.' Ava rolled her eyes. 'I remember being so excited when I found it.'

'You found it?' Paiges's mind went to the ring box in her bag. Why would Ava have buried it again.

'No, I mean, when I found it in his bedroom drawer. You remember, don't you? I showed it to you at college.'

'I remember.'

'We were such good friends, weren't we? I couldn't wait for you to see it. I still sometimes wonder what happened to that ring, you know.'

Paige sipped some tea to avoid Ava's eyes.

'I wonder who took it. Someone from college, I suppose. Or it could have just fallen out of my bag; I was always losing things. It was my own fault; I should never have taken it. Remember the time when I lost my house keys and we walked for about a mile looking for them?'

'Oh, yes. I'd forgotten about that.' Paige pondered what Ava had said, *"...or it could have just fallen out of my bag"; "It was my own fault."* All this time she'd been so worried and dejected about what she'd done, but Ava held no blame. Ava hadn't lost any sleep over it. *"It was my own fault; I should never have taken it."*

So many wasted years of wondering, so many wasted years of worry. All it would have taken was one conversation with Ava to ease her concerns. *"...or it could have just fallen out of my bag."*

It had never really mattered.

'Funny how the things we worry about as teenagers actually don't mean anything in the long run,' said Ava. 'James and I got married in the end, anyway.' She let out a laugh. 'Not immediately. It actually took us another twenty years or so. But we met up again not long after leaving college. We often joke about me losing the ring.'

'Oh, right...'

'It all kind of came together nicely, actually; James told me about his uncle who was retiring from the family business, and as we were both out of work at the time he said I could join him and work here until I found a job. I'm still here nearly thirty years later!'

'It all worked out well in the end,' said Paige, trying to sound upbeat while a million thoughts converged.

'I'm glad the ring was stolen,' continued Ava.

Paige's eyes widened at that.

'It was a blessing in disguise. It taught us something. We both found it so hard being apart and that was a great foundation for our marriage. We'll be celebrating our tenth wedding anniversary next month. We didn't get married straight away, we wanted to save up and have a special day. We should have invited you. I have the photos at home; you can come and see them. James will be thrilled to see you again.'

Paige smiled at Ava. On averting her eyes she noticed that Ava was wearing an engagement ring identical to the one she'd seen in the shop window; the one that looked the same as the ring Paige had taken and buried.

Ava followed her gaze. 'Look,' she said, holding out her left hand. 'This engagement ring is an exact replica of the one James's uncle made all those years ago when James was going to ask me to marry him. We love the design so much that we decided to sell it in the shop. It's one of our bestsellers. Who would have guessed back then, when I was stressing over losing the ring, that all this would have happened? Funny how life is, isn't it? Full of surprises. So tell me more about what you've been up to these past thirty-odd years, Paige.'

Gunshot

Pearl heard the gunshot but went back to sleep.

The unmistakable blast shook her awake and was followed by an ominous silence. She'd pulled the blanket closer, an uneasy feeling inside. It seemed wrong to ignore what she'd heard. Her husband, Grant, had somehow slept through the chilling noise. She didn't want to wake him, though, as he'd told her he had a long day of work ahead of him.

Pearl shut her eyes tightly and willed sleep to come to the rescue and take away her dilemma. Something like a scream sounded as she drifted off; the unconscious world of dream state took hold just in time, reality mercifully fading away for a while.

When Pearl awoke, however, reality returned and refused to be ignored: the first thing she heard was a police car pulling up noisily outside.

After shuffling over to the bedroom window, she pulled the curtains open, regret preying on her conscience. How much time had passed between the gunshot and the police car arriving remained unclear. Would it have made a difference if she'd called the police straight away, or woken Grant?

Grant's voice disturbed her musings, 'It's those idiots from next door again. Probably had another fight.'

'Did you hear anything last night?' she asked him gingerly.

'Only an owl.'

Pearl watched as two police officers approached the neighbours' house. 'Owls are supposed to be messengers of death, aren't they?'

'That's a bit dark for a Tuesday morning,' said Grant. 'Have you seen my green socks, love?'

'They're in the drawer.'

'Thanks. Apart from the owl, I heard you snoring,' he said, putting an arm around her.

Forcing a laugh, Pearl pulled away from his embrace. 'I heard a gunshot.'

'When?'

'Last night.'

'Guns at night in rural Hertfordshire?' Grant raised an eyebrow. 'You must've been dreaming, love.' He kissed her cheek.

Must have been dreaming. The words offered some respite but guilt soon resumed along with the echo of the gunshot.

'I'll be late home tonight,' he said. 'We have a staff meeting.'

9

'Yes, you said,' she mumbled. She watched him as he pulled on his socks oblivious to the world outside the window.

Turning back to survey the frantic scene, Pearl noticed an ambulance parked next to the police car. Although it wasn't unusual for the couple next door to argue and for the police to be called by worried neighbours, this sight was unusual for Serenity Close. A sizeable crowd of people—some of them neighbours, but some Pearl didn't recognise—were watching the door of number eleven with interest. Crime-scene tape added a sinister and disturbing quality to the spectacle. Pearl hadn't seen that tape in real life for many years, only on TV dramas and news articles; seeing it now brought back memories of when they were still living in London, the murder of a neighbour by a jealous boyfriend. The colour of blood and the sense of despair flashed in Pearl's mind as recollections burst forth.

Nothing ever really happened in Serenity Close, a peaceful cul-de-sac. They'd moved here to escape the uncertainty of living in over-populated London with the endless news of street crime overshadowing everything and making it harder to walk along any street without being on high alert the whole time.

The neighbours were relative strangers having only moved in about six months before. Grant commented at the time, 'They've moved here from London; let's hope they're not criminals, hey?'

Pearl had laughed it off. 'Huh, we came from London too, remember?'

'Yeah, I remember; that's why I said it. London's not the same as it was when we were young, Pearl.'

'It's not that bad. "If you're tired of London, you're tired of life", isn't that how the saying goes?'

'Don't tell me you're regretting moving away.'

'No. Well, not really. Sometimes it seems a bit quiet here, though, don't you think?'

'I prefer it.'

'Yeah, but you still work in London, so you get the best of both worlds.'

'Believe me, love, you're better off not having to battle through the crowds on endless commutes and deal with all the pollution.'

'Isn't there anything you like about London?'

'I like some things about it, but not the crime.'

As echoes of the conversation from the past resurged, Pearl spoke her thoughts: 'Looks like the crime has followed us here from London, Grant. There's no getting away from it.'

'This is the first time anything has happened here in nearly a year, Pearl. We used to hear about local crime every day when we were living in London.'

'Well, you're bound to get more crime where there are more people,' she said.

'Exactly. That's why we moved out here, remember? To get away from all the hustle and bustle. To enjoy the quiet life.'

Lines formed on Pearl's brow.

Something about Phillip—the man who lived next door—unsettled Pearl. He mostly presented as visibly on edge. On more than one occasion it had crossed her mind that he could be a drug-addict or alcoholic: he possessed a kind of jittery demeanour, as if craving his next high. He looked like a weightlifter; muscular and tall. She found herself purposefully avoiding having a conversation with him whenever their paths crossed, surprising herself with impromptu invented excuses.

He never initiated conversation, but somehow even a glance from him would cause a panic to rise inside her, so almost without thinking she'd reel off a reason why she couldn't stop to talk: 'I'm sorry, can't stop; I have to collect the children from a friend's house.'; 'Oh, is it that time already? I should be getting back to the kids.'; 'Sorry, I'm late for an appointment.'; 'I need to collect my mother from the hospital.' His eyes would exude relief and he'd noticeably relax when he heard her excuses, so that she was always left feeling awkward, questioning herself as to why she'd spoken at all.

Although a mysterious and evasive character in public, when indoors Phillip became very vocal: talking too loudly, shouting at his partner.

The walls between their properties were not well soundproofed so the couple's arguments filtered through. Pearl knew that just leaning closer to the wall would allow access to every word, but she invariably ended up increasing the volume on the television to drown out their altercations: there was something rather disconcerting about the way Phillip's voice boomed and how, in contrast, his wife's high-pitched and much quieter voice leaked a sense of anguish and torment through the paper-thin party wall.

Estelle, Phillip's wife, was a timid-looking woman. Pearl had chatted with her a few times; they'd talked about their gardens, the weather, and their children. Nothing more.

Estelle constantly seemed in a hurry to be somewhere else, mirroring how Pearl would act when face to face with Phillip; that same kind of urgency to get away. In the midst of conversation, Estelle appeared preoccupied; there'd be a faraway look in her eyes, consequently Pearl could never be sure whether the woman actually heard what she was saying.

Phillip and Estelle were an odd couple: he was tall and well-built, and she was under five feet in height and very slim, almost childlike. They had a twelve-year-old son, Nathan, who had grown taller than Estelle, his physique similar to his father's.

The policemen emerged from the house next door solemn-faced. They exchanged a few words, while one of them scribbled notes onto a pad of paper.

Paramedics, carrying a stretcher, were the next to walk out of the house. They appeared to be struggling to lift the stretcher, which held a large body shrouded in a sheet...

Phillip? Pearl held a hand in front of her mouth. *Estelle must have finally found the courage to stand up for herself... But where on earth would she have got a gun? Maybe he was trying to use it against her and she'd shot him in self-defence...*

Pearl turned around and saw that Grant had left the room. She called out to him, 'Grant, something terrible's happened!'

Her attention was drawn back to the goings-on in Serenity Close when she heard Estelle scream, 'He's only a child!'

A gasp left Pearl's lips. *No. Not Nathan.* Pearl looked at the stretcher, tears forming in her eyes as an image of the boy flashed into her mind; he was only a year older than her own son.

'He didn't mean to do it!' rang out Estelle's plea. 'It was an accident!'

Pearl's eyes widened as she struggled to understand. *How can she be defending him? Maybe he's threatened her, threatened to kill her too if she says anything against him...* Feeling sickened, she followed Estelle's anguished stare and then noticed the police car.

As he was being handcuffed and bundled into the vehicle, Nathan shouted over his shoulder, 'It wasn't an accident, Mum! I'm glad he's dead!'

Change of Heart

Angela couldn't remember; Gina could never forget.

⚜

Gina ran down the escalator, anxious to catch the Tube train that could be heard pulling into the platform. Pushing past a woman who was walking slowly, Gina huffed. *I need a coffee*, she thought, blaming exhaustion for the show of impatience. She'd missed breakfast because getting to work on time rated as more important, and she'd struggled to get out of bed due to lack of sleep.

The insomnia came about because of Bradley, or more accurately because of her expectation that he should reply to her text message; he hadn't responded. After their first date, Gina got carried away, imagining herself in a relationship with Bradley. There seemed to be a mutual attraction. Two months later, with little communication from him apart from the odd text or sporadic interaction on Facebook, she was starting to feel ignored.

Gina jumped onto the Tube train and turned around only to notice the slow-walking woman stepping into the carriage.

⚜

Angela looked at the young woman. *This must be her*, the thought came from out of nowhere, *the one I was warned about.* The girl had shoved her out of the way before boarding the train. *I have to do it now.* A feeling of despair took hold before all went black.

The knife—a small, serrated kitchen knife—had been plunged deep into Gina's shoulder, narrowly missing an artery.

'You're quite a lucky girl; must have had an angel on your shoulder, Miss Turner,' said the doctor. 'If it had just been... perhaps a centimetre to the left, you may not have survived to tell the tale.'

Lucky? Gina didn't feel lucky to have been stabbed by a deranged woman on a train. 'If I'd had an angel with me, surely they would've kept that crazy woman away from me.'

The doctor laughed but said nothing further.

One minute she'd been on the train, the next lying in a hospital bed. As the doctor relayed the story, pictures formed in Gina's mind: the stranger she'd pushed aside who'd subsequently boarded the train; the woman's hollow stare. Gina remembered feeling intimidated. It all happened so quickly. Gina turned around to avoid the hard stare; the woman seemed angry. Then there were screams. For a short while Gina stood still, stunned, watching people screaming, confused by their reactions... Did a terrorist board the train? Maybe someone with a gun, or someone with a belt of explosives?

'Are you all right?' asked a fellow passenger, his eyes wide as he looked at Gina. Then he'd called out to the other passengers: 'Quick, someone call an ambulance... Pull the alarm! We need something for the wound, to stem the flow...'

Gina lowered her gaze and noticed the blood... everywhere. Her eyes were drawn to the woman holding a bloody knife in her hand. Then nothing.

☦

Lying on the hospital bed, Gina thought back over the events of the morning. She had been in such a hurry to get to work. It all seemed so unimportant now. No one should have to work 9 to 5 these days, but Sue, her boss, was unforgiving about lateness. She'd reported one of Gina's colleagues to HR the year before when he arrived at work fifteen minutes late, and he had almost lost his job. Sue often strolled into the office after 10 a.m. and left early, but the staff were not given any flexibility.

Gina noticed the time; it was nearly ten o'clock. She hadn't phoned the office to let them know where she was. An image formed in her mind's eye: Sue looking at the clock, cheeks reddening, nose up in the air as usual. 'Does anyone know where Gina is?' Gina pushed the thought away and sneered. Sue was to blame for all of it, creating the paranoia about being late resulting in her frenzied impatience to board the train. If she hadn't been in such a rush, she wouldn't have pushed past that woman, and that woman wouldn't have reacted in the way she did. She felt a shiver as she recalled the stranger's eyes staring through her before she'd approached her and pulled the knife.

☦

'Yes. I definitely saw a young woman. I can still see her face if I close my eyes; she practically shoved me aside to get onto the train. I remember thinking that young people have no patience these days.' Angela looked down at her hands.

'You were angered because she pushed you?' asked the doctor.

'I wouldn't say *angered*. Maybe a bit shaken up. I don't remember anything after boarding the train. I remember stepping into the carriage, but nothing more. I'd assumed I must have passed out.'

'You were carrying a knife.'

'A small kitchen knife,' explained Angela, 'to use at lunchtime. I also had a fork and a spoon. I take my own cutlery to work, don't trust the hygiene in the office kitchen.'

'So, you don't remember anything after boarding the train?'

'Nothing at all.'

'It seems as if it was a psychotic episode. Have you ever suffered from mental illness in the past?' The psychiatrist waited for an answer.

'No,' Angela lied. It still persisted, the sense of shame. She'd suffered a breakdown many years ago, in her mid-twenties, and spent time in a psychiatric ward. Family and friends drifted away after the episode. Angela was aware that their departure from her life was a reaction caused by fear or ignorance, but it didn't stop her feelings of inadequacy.

Times had changed; mental illness wasn't as much of a taboo subject these days, but even being aware of that could not shift Angela's ingrained lack of inner worth, so entrenched; the idea of revealing the truth, exposing herself, struck her as more daunting a prospect than facing a mountain with an unreachable summit.

Whenever the depression threatened, which it had done quite frequently over the years, she'd found ways to keep it at bay.

Angela often saw herself as more of an onlooker in life, just outside, not fully involved. Friends and colleagues would get excited about things, plan ahead; she'd constantly feel stuck, tormented. Her heightened tension had morphed into a familiar companion, like an old comfort blanket a child might become attached to; it felt safer to stay within its hold. The dark feeling—usually depicted in comics and animation as a black cloud and, ironically, often in a jokey way—remained like an obtrusive shadow, forever present in Angela's life, at least on the periphery of consciousness. She kept it to herself. Didn't want to be labelled, didn't want the stigma.

'We'll have to keep you here for a while and do some tests,' the doctor explained.

'Is she all right? The girl?' Even while asking the question, Angela wasn't sure she wanted to know the answer. Anxiety began to play its mind-games, concocting the worst-case scenario. The girl could be dead or permanently disabled. Flashes of courtrooms, police stations, jail cells, came to mind along with the familiar sense of being guilty, blaming herself for everything.

'She'll be fine, Ms Mobrey.'

The doctor's words battled against Angela's inner anguish. Was he telling the truth or trying to protect a fragile mind?

'It could have been much worse,' continued the psychiatrist. 'We have to make sure you're fit to leave, to avoid anything like this happening again.'

'Will I go to prison?'

'We believe it was mental illness, so we are going to present a report to the court. It's a very serious incident.'

'Why can't I remember any of it?'

The doctor's eyes gave nothing away. Did it sound believable? Wouldn't it be best to tell the truth? It was all there in her medical records, after all.

'It's quite unusual for someone your age to do this type of thing, Ms Mobrey, without any history of mental illness. Although, it's not beyond the realms of probability that it was some kind of episode maybe linked to trauma.'

'I lied.'

'I'm not sure what you're saying, Ms Mobrey. Please elaborate. Are you telling me you deliberately stabbed that girl?'

'No; no, I wouldn't do anything like that... I lied about... I do have a history of mental illness.'

With some coaxing from the doctor and many tears, Angela began to open up, unlocking the secrets that were buried deep under years of insecurities, scraping away the untruths, revealing what lay beneath.

Talking about the past felt freeing somehow. The doctor wasn't being judgemental. He seemed to find it interesting, was asking many questions. It felt almost as if her experience was helping him to learn more. The weight of carrying it all inside for so long slid away bit by bit. The doctor didn't react in horror, but with sympathy, giving her hope and explaining the help they could offer.

'Don't worry. You're not alone. We can help you. In fact, if you'd seen a doctor sooner, chances are this incident might never have happened.'

❦

There'd been an outpouring of sympathy on Facebook. Nothing from Bradley. At first, Gina obsessed over that, almost ignoring all the positive messages. Now, nearly two weeks later, there was still no word from him. Today it didn't matter: her perspective had changed. The days laid up in a hospital bed offered the gift of time to contemplate what was important.

Gina heard that the woman who'd stabbed her had been admitted to hospital, suffering from mental illness. Reflecting on her own behaviour, Gina couldn't help wondering how much of what she'd done had provoked the woman's reaction. Things could have turned out much worse. Gina had expected to feel angry about what happened, but somehow there'd been a mental shift.

Gina walked towards the Tube station platform. Her first day back at work since the "accident". The doctor at the hospital had given her a leaflet about the symptoms of Post Traumatic Stress Disorder.

Gina took deep breaths, trying to keep her nervousness under control. She walked more slowly than usual and observed the other commuters. Many appeared to be in a rush, oblivious to other people's needs or existence. Huffing and tutting down escalators and along platforms, cursing everyone around them, the commuters conveniently forgot the real reason for their lateness: they'd set off on their journeys at the last possible moment thereby giving themselves only a limited amount of time to get to where they were going. In this moment, with one-track minds, it was always the person in front of them that was to blame for their slow progress. Always someone else to blame.

The world was moving at a faster pace and people were caught up in it all, too busy to care. She noticed a man shaking his head impatiently as a woman in front of him struggled to place her suitcase on the escalator. These were the tiny sparks of anger that trickled all year round and led to arguments, led to violence, spiralled into social degeneration. The man didn't offer to help the woman with her suitcase, but rushed past her as soon as she was on the escalator, reminding Gina of the way she had pushed past the older woman a couple of weeks before.

Does it always have to take a tragic or traumatic event to change people? Gina wondered. Just slowing down, taking a deep breath, taking a step back, could avoid so much pain. Such a simple idea, but so difficult to grasp.

There was a man with a walking stick in front of Gina on the station platform, moving very slowly.

The train arrived.

Gina stood and waited for the man to reach the door of the carriage. 'Do you need any help?' she asked, with a smile.

'Yes, please dear,' he smiled back.

Gina thought again of the woman who'd stabbed her, and hoped she'd be all right.

In the Past

'Your name, sir?' the question repeated with more force, impatience seeping from the receptionist's eyes.

'Um... I'm here for an interview at two o'clock with Mr Squires; you should have my name.' That would sound rude, wouldn't it? He'd already tried the receptionist's patience. His mind had gone blank. Panic set in; he had never forgotten his name before. Perspiration formed on his brow as the seconds ticked away.

'Roger Bainsford?' she huffed. 'I'll just check whether Mr Squires is back from lunch. Take a seat.'

Roger breathed a sigh of relief and walked over to the Chesterfield sofa. He sat facing the door, to avoid looking at the receptionist and prayed she didn't have a say in the recruitment process; he needed this job. He'd been unemployed for three months and was fighting a custody battle with his ex-wife. Their eight-year-old son, Jeremy, had been living with him since the divorce, but he'd lost his last job due to consistent lateness. He'd found it hard to get Jeremy ready for school and get to work on time. His ex-wife was doing everything she could to try to persuade the the court that Jeremy should be living with her.

'Mr Bainsford, Mr Squires will see you now,' said the receptionist. She then turned back to her computer and began tapping away at the keyboard.

Roger stood up and approached the desk. 'Um... excuse me, Miss, which room?'

'Straight up the stairs, first door on the left,' she said without looking at him.

He walked away and up the steep staircase. When he reached the door, he tapped it lightly, nerves jangling. The gold-plated letters on the door plaque read: **Paul Squires, Managing Director.** Ever since receiving the letter from the company offering an interview, he'd wondered whether the managing director was the same Paul Squires he'd once known. If he was, he prayed he wouldn't remember him.

Five years ago, Roger had called Paul a vile drunk who deserved to die; harsh words spoken in anger, but spoken nonetheless. They'd been at a mutual friend's stag do and Paul drank too much alcohol. Roger had been warned by Scott (the groom-to-be) that Paul could get a bit rowdy when drunk.

Paul revealed to Roger he was planning to persuade everyone to strip Scott to his underpants at the end of the night and tie him to a lamppost, which he said was customary. Roger refused to be involved and resolved to hang around and untie Scott if the worst happened.

Paul and Roger had bickered throughout the evening, and as they were all getting into a taxi to go home Paul punched Roger in the face, causing a nosebleed. Paul just laughed. The others managed to calm Roger down and blamed it on the drink.

After the rest of the group had been dropped off at their respective homes, Roger and Paul were the last two remaining in the cab. Roger tried to ignore Paul, who appeared to be dozing off. Then, without warning, Paul sat up and peered at Roger: 'I know who you are now,' he'd said. 'I've been trying to place your face all night.'

Roger felt sure he was about to say something absurd with the intention of starting another argument—he was certain he'd never met Paul before.

'You're Roger Bainsford, aren't you? Used to go to Prichester primary school. You've a little sister, Sally.'

'Er... yeah... How—'

'I was known as Paul Simms back then; my mum divorced and changed my name.'

'Paul Simms?'

'Yeah. You remember?'

'You stole my lunch money, made Sally cry.'

'Ha, ha! That's the one.' Paul guffawed. 'Don't worry, though, I made it up to Sally a few years later. We had a bit of a fling, y'know. She was well up for it. Only fifteen.'

Roger glared at Paul.

'Look, mate, don't take my word for it, ask her.'

'She wouldn't look twice at a loser like you,' blurted Roger. 'Let's end this conversation before you regret opening your mouth.'

'Tough words. You were a bit of a wimp at school, I seem to recall.'

'I know what you're trying to do. People like you are always looking for a fight.'

'It's all true, though, me and Sally. But, hey, c'mon, let's forget all that... It was in the past... we were kids. What d'ya say we go to a strip club? It's still early.'

'It's two in the morning.'

'Yeah, like I said, early.' Paul began to laugh, then retched and ended up being sick in the back of the cab.

'Bloody hell, I'll charge you extra for that!' shouted the taxi driver.

They reached Paul's house and he stepped out of the cab. 'See you later, alligator. He's paying,' he said as he waved at Roger and stuck up a middle finger.

That's when Roger had told him he deserved to die.

How did a useless drunk end up Managing Director of this place? Roger shook his head and pushed open the office door. Surely it couldn't be the same man. If it was *that* Paul Squires, he'd never have invited him for an interview. Or would he? Did he have some kind of bitter revenge planned?

Recognition registered on Paul's face as soon as Roger entered the room. He smiled broadly and stood up. 'Well, well, well, we meet again, Roger Bainsford. As you can see, I am still very much alive.'

'I... '

'No need to apologise. I deserved it. Always did feel bad about making you pay for that taxi.' He laughed. 'It seems our paths were meant to cross many times in this lifetime.'

Roger braced himself. His entire being was screaming to leave, but he couldn't afford to be unemployed any longer and this was the first job interview he'd secured in three months. Cursing his luck, he sat opposite Paul and said, 'Listen, before we start, I'm sorry about what I said to you after Scott's stag do. It was rude and wrong; I was a bit drunk myself.'

Paul held up a hand and frowned. 'No apology necessary, I was the one in the wrong. I punched you. I'm surprised you didn't hit me back. Shows your good nature. Your CV's impressive. I have to say, I was wondering if it would be awkward meeting up, but actually it's quite nice.'

Roger forced a smile, not sure where the conversation was leading.

'I've always fancied running a family business, and you have all the experience I need,' continued Paul.

'A family business?'

'I bumped into your sister last month. We're kind of seeing each other again. She mentioned about you being out of work.'

'Sally? She's the one who suggested I should apply here.'

'I suggested it to her, actually. As I say, it'd be nice to have a family business.'

'But...'

'Oh, don't worry, I've cleaned myself up. Haven't had a drink for two years this May. That night in the cab kind of brought it home to me, I was really going off the rails. Seeing you again after all that time made me think, you know. I started to think about who I used to be, what I'd become, what I really wanted from life. Took me a while, but I picked myself up and here I am. You said I was a vile drunk, a loser—'

'I didn't mean—'

'Please don't apologise. I needed to hear it. I wouldn't be where I am today if someone like you hadn't made me take a long hard look at

20

myself, I'm grateful. So, when can you start?'

Family Ties

'You can't just force us to stay here!' yelled Margaret, finding her voice, having been silent ever since being brought to the house.

'Shut up and sit down. I'm your father and you'll listen to me.'

'You're not my father!'

'One more word from you and you'll go to bed without any supper.'

The storm in his eyes frightened Margaret, so she decided to sit down. Looking around the room, she wondered why no one else was protesting. There were four of them and only one of him. There were no chains binding them. He hadn't locked the door. How did he hold such power over them? He didn't even have a weapon. There was the threat: he'd said that if any of them tried to leave he'd kill their loved ones. Why did they all so readily believe him?

He was at least middle-aged, with a balding head sprouting a few grey strands around the sides, and a long, unkempt beard, reddish-brown in colour. His eyes were grey, and red veins flecked the whites, making it appear as though he hadn't slept in days. He kept checking his mobile phone, seemed edgy, fidgety.

What could he be planning to do with them?

Miranda raised a hand; a slight girl, maybe nine years old, with extremely long blonde hair that had probably never seen a pair of scissors. Her eyes were red from crying; she'd hardly stopped snivelling and asking for her mother.

'What is it, Miranda?' huffed the man.

'Can I go to the toilet?'

'Yes, but be quick. And no games or I'll kill your family.'

That threat again.

When Miranda returned, the man ordered them all to sit around a large table at the rear of the kitchen.

Margaret turned her attention to the others: Miranda continued to snivel; Kevin appeared sad but kept quiet—he looked about eight years old, in Margaret's estimation. Janice was the eldest of the captives, a twenty-something girl whose deep frown hadn't shifted for even a moment.

Janice and Kevin had already been in the house when Margaret arrived. Margaret was still quite shaken up by how the man had captured her so easily. He had followed her when she was leaving school, approached her from behind, blindfolding her and placing something over her mouth, so she couldn't scream out for help. She'd been bundled into the back of a van. The drive had taken a long time, but she wondered whether in her mind it had taken longer because she was so frightened. He hadn't said a word to her the whole time, so she had no idea who had taken her, was it a man, a woman, more than one person? Where was she being taken? The fear of what could happen raced through her mind creating terrifying images of the worst kinds of eventualities. She was too shocked to cry or even to move. She remained frozen, as if staying in one position would save her from whatever fate had in store. On arriving at the house, she'd been locked in a room on her own, still blindfolded, while he went to fetch Miranda. She knew Janice was there though because she kept shouting out from another room, 'Hello! Can anyone hear me?' Margaret had remained silent, still, suspicious that whoever was calling out might be somehow complicit in her abduction.

An hour or so after she'd arrived she now sat around the imposing large oak table with the others. Their captor was at the head of the table, two of them on either side.

'You're probably all wondering why I've brought you here,' said the man. 'Let me start by introducing myself. My name's Max Robins. Janice, you can call me Max. I'm your husband. You are Mrs Robins now.'

Janice gasped and then retched.

'Don't act so shocked. You'll get used to it.' Max rolled his eyes. 'The rest of you will call me Dad. I'm your new dad. Again, you'll get used to it.'

Miranda began to cry. 'I want my mum.'

'Jan love, see to the child. Janice is your new mum, everyone. You'll get used to that too.'

'I don't know what you're trying to do, but this is weird. I'm leaving,' said Margaret. Although her legs were shaking she stood up. 'You can't hold us here.' She hurried towards the kitchen door.

'If you have any sense, you'll return to the table. I have my people watching your parents' home. If you leave, they'll be dead within minutes.'

Margaret thought of her mum and dad. Was he bluffing? She still had her mobile phone; perhaps she could send them a text when his back was turned. Warn them. Tell them to leave the house.

'We're going to have fun. It's an experiment.' Max peered around the table through squinted eyes.

'You can't just round people up for an experiment, we're not mice!' screamed Margaret, at her wits' end.

'Well, you see,' Max pointed a spindly finger at Margaret, 'it's just

23

that kind of thinking that proves to me you deserve to be here. *Need* to be here. You haven't been raised right. Mice have feelings too, you know.'

Margaret covered her face with her hands and breathed out in exasperation. Finally, she turned around and sat back down at the kitchen table.

'There, you see. You're starting to understand,' said Max. 'We're going to be living together as a family.'

'This is crazy. You're crazy!' Margaret's voice was shaking but she was determined to try to escape. 'We're not a family, we don't even know each other.'

'You teenagers think you're so clever these days, don't you? So, tell us, Maggie, what does family mean to you?'

'My name's Margaret, not Maggie. And my family is my mum and dad, who are at home and expecting me to return there.'

'I don't have a dad,' said Kevin.

It was the first time she'd heard him speak since he arrived, Margaret noted. She empathised, realising that it would have taken some courage for him to speak up, given his age. She, herself, had been terrified.

'I'm your dad,' said Max.

'Are you my real dad?' asked Kevin.

'Yes,' said Max.

'So you came to get me? I knew you would. Mum said you left us and you never loved us.'

'Oh, shut up boy. I'm not *that* dad. I'm a new one. I have no idea who your actual dad was. He probably left because you were so annoying.'

'I was only two years old when he left.'

'That's the worst age. They call it "Terrible Twos", don't they? No wonder he left.'

'Why are we here?' asked Miranda between sniffles.

'I'm sixty-five next June and I've never known what it's like to have a family,' explained Max. 'Have you any idea what that feels like? You may all feel hard done by because I've taken you from your homes, but believe me, your suffering is nothing compared to the social exclusion, loneliness, and suffering I have endured my whole life.'

'Oh, this is ridiculous!' snapped Janice. 'I won't stand for it, I'm calling the police.' She took her phone from her jacket pocket.

Margaret felt herself breathe with relief now that she was not the only one challenging the man. She hoped that Janice, as she was older, would think of a way to get them out of there.

'Go on, call the police, but if you do, your family will be dead before they get here. My people are watching your house.' Max looked around at the others with a piercing scowl. 'They're watching all of your houses. One false move and you will know what it's like to have no family.'

Janice dropped her phone onto the wooden table.

Margaret let out a frustrated sigh on seeing Janice's reaction. 'You keep saying *your people*. If you don't have a family and were so isolated and lonely, who are these people?' she blurted, hoping to bolster Janice's confidence.

'They are a group of criminals I met in prison. I was in there for quite some time. I killed some people in the past.'

'This doesn't make sense,' said Janice as she retrieved her phone with a shaky hand.

'Life doesn't make sense,' said Max.

'When you say you don't have a family, what happened to them? Did you kill them?' asked Janice, fear in her eyes.

'No. I never had a family. I was sent to an orphanage at a young age. Story was, my parents were killed in a war somewhere, I never found out the details. I had a few foster parents but none of them lasted long, they didn't want the burden of an unhappy child. When I was a teenager, I ran away from a care home and lived rough for years. I got into a few fights, killed a few people and ended up in jail. I was released about a year ago and given housing by the local council. This place. I just want a normal life. Wife, kids.'

'This is about as far from normal as you could get,' said Margaret.

'You can't force people to be your family,' snapped Janice. 'I sympathise with your story, but I can't condone this. Look at these children, they're terrified. Our families will be looking for us. You won't get away with this.'

'Maybe not, but unlike you I have nothing to lose, which brings me back to my earlier point: I doubt any of you can claim to have faced anything close to the suffering I've been through. You all have idyllic lives compared to mine.'

'My mum's dying,' said Miranda, still sniffling.

Max remained silent.

Margaret sensed a flicker of compassion in his gaze; would he release the girl?

'She might be dead within weeks. She's only been given a month by her doctor. I want to see her,' blubbered Miranda.

'Forget them. They're your past. You have a new family here. Janice is your mum now. Maybe this is God's way of making sure you're cared for. I mean, who would look after you after your mum dies?'

'My dad.'

'I'm your dad, remember?'

Miranda stood up. 'No, you're not!' She headed for the door.

'Go home! I didn't want a snivelling wreck of a daughter, anyway. I'll be fine with my Kevin and Maggie.'

Miranda ran out of the room.

'How will she get home?' asked Janice. 'She's only a child. Maybe I should take her.'

'I could go with her,' said Margaret, seeing this as an opportunity to finally get away.

'Nice try,' said Max. 'No one else is leaving here.'

'I'm supposed to collect my daughter from school today,' complained Janice. 'Can I at least call my husband and let him know he has to collect her? I won't say anything else.'

'No. I think you should all give me your phones. No more access to the outside world until you get used to being my family. And don't think you can resist. I have a gun on me. Max collected their phones forcibly and placed them in a cupboard above the kitchen sink, locking the door.

'Our families will be looking for us,' repeated Janice in a little voice. Margaret could tell she was afraid of the man; she'd been counting on Janice, being the eldest, to somehow get them out, but now her hopes were dwindling.

'You keep saying your family is looking for you,' snarled Max. 'Perhaps they're happy you're gone, have you considered that?'

'My mum won't care,' said Kevin. 'She takes drugs and has lots of boyfriends. Most of the time I have to take care of myself.'

Max frowned. 'You mean you prefer being here?'

'Yeah,' said Kevin. 'I always wanted a dad. I think you'll look after me, won't you?'

'I don't need that kind of responsibility.'

'Um... dads have to take responsibility for children under sixteen,' stated Janice, seeming to have recovered a bit of her courage.

'Yes, but I was expecting someone from a normal family, not a kid who's so clingy.'

'You obviously have no idea what a normal family is,' said Janice. 'Most families put up with each other because they love each other. By sending Miranda away, you showed that you don't know what a family is. If you were her real dad, you wouldn't have sent her away. And if you were Kevin's dad, you would be glad to look after him. I think your little *family* experiment is failing.'

'Janice you are my wife and you will not speak to me like that. A wife has to respect her husband.'

'Respect is a two way street,' she snapped.

'Women these days, you don't know your place.'

'I know my place isn't here. I really should be getting back to my family.' Janice stood up.

'Me too,' said Margaret, feeling braver now that Janice was standing up for herself; maybe they could overpower him.

'You're going nowhere,' growled Max. 'We are a family and you are part of it.'

'I want you to stay,' said Kevin.

'See? Listen to the boy. He needs you.'

'This is ridiculous. Kevin, dear, you do understand that this man is some kind of criminal and he's holding us here against our will, don't you?' said Janice, gently, leaning towards Kevin.

Max snorted, 'I only rounded you lot up so that I have people to look after me. That's why I picked older kids rather than toddlers. I need people who will be my family and defend me. I can't work, or claim benefits, I'm underground. I need people to support me. I'm on the run. There was some old fella living here when I escaped from prison, I killed him.'

Janice gasped.

'Don't look so surprised. You know my background.'

'This doesn't make any sense at all,' said Margaret, losing her patience. She stood up. 'You brought us here to live with you so that we could look after you, pay the bills, buy your food? You haven't thought it through, though. The police will be looking for you and our families are looking for us.'

'Your families will never find you because we're miles away from any of them.'

'It's okay, I want to be here,' said Kevin. 'It's better than home. I'm glad I have a dad to look after me now. You'll stay forever won't you, Dad?'

'What?' Max stood up. 'I think you should go home, Kevin, your mum needs you more than I do.' He returned Kevin's phone to him.

'But you said you were my dad.'

'I lied.'

Max led Kevin out of the room, practically pushing him outside. 'Some family this is turning out to be,' he moaned. 'Oh well, at least I have a wife and a daughter to support me.'

'Will Miranda and Kevin be all right? What about your *people*? The ones watching their houses,' asked Janice.

'Don't worry about them, they only act on my instructions.'

There was a loud knock on the front door. It repeated after a short moment and a man's voice called: 'Max Robins? Police. Open up.'

'Police? Duck, you two. Go into the bedroom and hide under the bed, or in the wardrobe. If you don't, your families will die. If not today, as soon as I get out of prison.'

Margaret thought this would be a perfect moment to escape, but Janice took Margaret's hand and led her to the bedroom.

Margaret listened with interest from the bedroom as the front door opened.

'Mr Robins, we understand you are holding three people against their will.'

'You can't enter without a search warrant.'

'Is that a confession?'

'I don't know what you're talking about.'

Margaret heard Miranda's voice. 'They're in there,' said Miranda, pointing towards the kitchen.

'We can go now,' whispered Margaret to Janice. 'There's police out there with Miranda. He can't hurt us.' She took Janice's hand.

Max's voice boomed from the front of the house. 'Come in and have a look, if you must.' His voice then sounded from the kitchen area. 'See? No one here. That girl is slightly crazy, I think. I'm not sure what she was doing here earlier. She came here and claimed to be my daughter, then when I told her to leave, she said she was going to tell the police. She's completely bonkers if you ask me.'

Margaret and Janice emerged from the bedroom.

One of the police officers proceeded to place handcuffs on Max. 'We've been looking for you. Let's get you back to prison, hey?'

The other officer explained, 'Mr Robins escaped from prison on a parole day. He won't be getting any more of those for the foreseeable future.'

Max sneered at the girls over his shoulder. 'What are you gawping at? Call yourselves family? You're traitors! I'm better off alone.'

The Games People Play

Lucas sat opposite his wife of twenty years, Penny, at the kitchen table. His eyes drifted to the calendar on the wall. Below the snow-capped mountain scene on the calendar, the days of the month were listed: December. Christmas loomed large. Lucas hated Christmas.

Penny crunched her cornflakes. After swallowing a mouthful, she cleared her throat and said, as if restraining a snarl, 'This year you're spending Christmas at home, right?'

'I'm sorry, honey.'

'It's been three years since you spent Christmas at home. Three years.' She raised her eyebrows. 'I swear I'm going to have a word with your boss.'

'I have to work—'

'No. No, you don't. Ask for time off.' Penny's searing look dared him to refuse.

'I can't—'

'I've been saying it to you all year: save your annual leave for Christmas—'

'It doesn't work like that—'

'Maybe you don't want to spend Christmas with us, is that it?' Her eyes glistened, as if she might cry.

'Don't be ridiculous,' said Lucas, while focussing on his empty cereal bowl; avoiding her gaze. 'Do you think I want to work on Christmas Day? The rest of the staff are away, so I have to cover.'

'Can't they just close for Christmas like everyone else?'

'We have important clients who expect us to be available.'

Penny looked down at the table. 'You're missing the best years of our children's lives, do you know that?'

'I'll be home on the twenty-eighth.'

'Why don't you get another job? You don't like working there anyway; you're always complaining about the long hours.'

'It's not that easy. Do you know how lucky we are that I even have a job in a recession?'

Lucas felt like he was repeating a script; it didn't mean anything. The lies were built on top of other lies. He didn't even have a job.

That evening, Lucas sat at a table in an expensive restaurant, but not with

Penny. With Elayna. Spending time alone with twenty-something Elayna was invigorating and refreshing. She didn't nag, just wanted to have fun. He'd met her at a time in his life when he needed an escape, as if stuck in a hole unable to fathom a way out. He knew it probably wasn't the most sensible thing to do, to start another affair, but he got carried away by her youthfulness.

At forty-five, and feeling slightly old, it boosted his ego to know that this young girl wanted to date him. She'd already said that she loved him: so innocent; yet to discover that love was an elusive fallacy, a playground for fools—a path leading only to disappointment or infinite loneliness, and that's if you're one of the lucky ones.

His mind drifted briefly to the past, as it regularly did, and the familiar sense of despair returned: a flashback to the end of his relationship with Olivia; unruly blonde locks tumbled over her face, her cheeks flushed. Lucas had been twenty-one; a mere child compared to the man who had stolen her from him. 'I'm sorry,' she'd mouthed, as if her voice did not wish to conspire in the deception. She'd scrabbled for the bedsheets to hide her nakedness. The man beside her in their bed had simply smiled apologetically. Lucas had often wondered whether he would so easily have cheated on Olivia. He knew the answer but it hurt too much to face it. He'd loved Olivia from the moment they met, when he sat next to her on the first day of secondary school. He'd lost himself in her sea-blue eyes for an eternal moment. Love at first sight was a phrase he'd heard a few times, and one he associated with their meeting.

Lucas shook the memories away.

'So, when can I meet your family?' asked Elayna, forcing Lucas's mind back to the present.

Lucas thought of Penny and the children. They were his family—well, the first thing that he thought of when anyone mentioned "family"—yet he knew the truth was *far* more complicated.

Elayna obviously meant she wanted to meet his parents when she said "family".

'It's still early days, Elayna,' he said, taking hold of her hand from across the table in the dimly-lit restaurant.

'But we've been dating for months. I want to meet your parents so that they can show me embarrassing photos of you as a child and tell me about all the crazy stuff you used to get up to.' She followed that with a giggle.

Lucas felt nostalgic for simpler times. These days there were far too many responsibilities to juggle. He brushed off Elayna's request with, 'That's precisely why I don't want you to meet them.'

'Oh, come on, let's spend Christmas at your parents', or even mine.' Her broad smile once again reminded him of how complicated his life had become, and the mention of Christmas brought to mind Penny's morning rant.

'I've told you, darling, I'm working through the Christmas period.'

'That's so unfair. How about New Year?'

'Um... yes, maybe New Year. Why don't we fly out to Paris? Would you like that?'

'Oh, wow! I'd love that!'

Lucas made a mental note to book a flight. He counted the days on his fingers under the table. *I'll have to lie to Penny about having to work over New Year as well.* If he spent a couple of days with Penny and the children—28th and 29th—he should be able to fly out to Paris for three days and be back before anyone noticed.

༄ঞ❧

Penny was washing the dishes when Lucas returned home later that evening.

'Where have you been?'

'Working late. Sorry, love.' He kissed her on the cheek.

'The kids are asleep. You hardly see them. Josh will be starting university next year, and Lucy is nearly sixteen. You're like a stranger to them.'

'You act as if I never see them. I see them most evenings. And let's face it, they're teenagers; it's hard to have a conversation with either of them without saying something that annoys them, all those hormones flying around.'

'That just shows that you don't know your children. Lucy and Josh are both decent kids, thank God. You need to spend more time with them.'

'I'll try,' he mumbled.

Penny glanced at him: 'Listen, I've been thinking about what we were talking about this morning. Why don't we go to my parents' for New Year? They're getting old, and they'd love to see the kids. We could drive up there and stay with them for a few days.'

Lucas bowed his head as he remembered Elayna's excitement about travelling to Paris. 'Sorry, Penny. Didn't I tell you I'm working that week? I thought I said. I'm home on the twenty-eighth and twenty-ninth, though. We'll have loads of quality time together then.'

Penny spun around, wet washing-up gloves leaving trails of bubbles on the floor: 'How can we call ourselves a family if we live separate lives?'

'You're getting everything out of proportion, darling. Christmas and New Year... it's commercial exploitation. Hard-working people like us being forced to spend money we don't have on things we don't need. We're together enough throughout the year, aren't we? Stop concentrating on one week in December... It's one week in a whole year.'

'You just don't get it, do you? Families are supposed to be together at Christmas. It's traditional. And, how can you say we spend enough time with each other when you travel abroad for work most weekends? Not to mention those evenings when you have to do extra shifts. Lucas, I mean it: you need to quit that job.'

'But the children will be off to university soon. There are fees to be paid. Not to mention all the latest gadgets that they're constantly asking for. How can we afford all that if I don't work?'

'I'm not saying don't work, all I'm saying is get a job that doesn't demand so much of your time.'

'Huh! A job like that wouldn't pay much.'

Penny shook her head and carried on washing the dishes in silence.

❦

Lucas sat in his parked car for a few minutes feeling quite exhausted. Penny's words had played on his mind all night. His conscience awakened to the harsh realisation that he hardly knew his two older children. He felt awkward when alone in a room with either of them, unsure what to say.

He'd almost called Josh "Peter" the week before. Peter was his younger son. He remembered back to his relatively uncomplicated life, when Josh and Lucy were toddlers; he'd been a loving father and faithful husband in those days. His life had changed dramatically. The man he'd become bore no resemblance to his former self.

A recollection emerged; something Olivia had once said. They'd talked about having children together. *You'd be such a great dad.'* He yearned to reach back in time, salvage the future that he'd imagined when he'd seen her face; the happy future idealised by the naïve perception of youth. All too soon, the memory was eclipsed, just like his former dreams. The image transformed into a black and white hazy picture of that night when Lucas returned home from university earlier than expected, to find Olivia in bed with the stranger; a man who'd haunted Lucas's mind ever since—a man without a name, without a personality, without anything but a face and a wry smile. He'd never come into contact with him again, but their liaison with Olivia was a common bond that linked them eternally. Lucas used to hate that man but could now only feel indifference, ruefully acknowledging that they were probably more alike than they were different.

He got out of his car and headed up the pathway at just after 7 a.m. Penny thought he'd gone to work.

As he walked in through the front door of Loulla's house, she greeted him dressed only in a slinky black négligée. He admired her slim figure.

They embraced, and shared a kiss.

'I've missed you,' she whispered.

'Me too,' he replied.

'I've got half an hour before I have to get ready for work. Let's not waste it.' She took his hand and led him upstairs to the bedroom.

Lucas lay in bed staring at the ceiling after Loulla left for work; soon he'd have to leave. He found the early mornings torturous, and it became increasingly difficult to keep track of where he should be each day.

He thought back to yesterday afternoon when he'd been at the park with Peter, his three-year-old, and his youngest child, one-year-old Julie. Their mother, Sally, worked full time. She loved her job, so it'd suited her when he'd offered to take care of the children during the day. He would go to Loulla's house first thing most mornings, and then when she left for work he'd go to Sally's.

Evenings were trickier: at first he used to have a meal with Sally when she got home from work, but one day she queried how he made it through the week with no sleep. As far as she knew, he looked after the children by day and then worked at night (like Loulla, Sally thought he worked a night shift at the local bakery). They agreed that it would be better if he got some sleep before his shift, so he came up with a story about how the bakery provided beds for staff, and said he preferred to sleep there rather than at home, to avoid being awoken by the children crying. Somehow she went along with this. It freed him to spend time with his other women in the evenings when Sally returned home from work.

Yesterday, he'd taken the toddlers to the park and met a pretty, young, single mother, Debbie. He'd seen her at the park before but they'd never talked to each other. After he introduced himself to her as a single parent, she'd suggested, while fluttering her eyelashes, that they meet for dinner one evening. The attraction was mutual and he contemplated taking her up on the offer of a date, but wondered how he could fit her in.

Most evenings he spent with Penny and the children, except the odd evening when he saw Elayna or Loulla. Weekends were mainly spent with Sally and the younger kids; he told Penny he had to fly abroad for work. He'd somehow managed to lie to Sally too by saying he had to care for his sick father some weekends, so he'd be able to spend some time with Penny. Now and then he really did fly abroad for a weekend, to visit Delphine, his lover in Paris. It was no coincidence that he'd suggested New Year in Paris to Elayna; he planned to sneak out and see Delphine at some point too.

Merely thinking about his schedule often brought on a headache.

On more than one occasion he'd been questioned by one or other of the women about his whereabouts on such and such a day. Fabricating a reasonable excuse always proved difficult. Penny left him speechless one evening by asking, 'Do you have a secret family hidden away somewhere?' Somehow he'd kept his composure. She'd brushed over her question, as if it were merely a flippant comment said in frustration; she didn't appear to actually suspect anything. It unnerved him, just the same.

Sally also said a similar thing recently: 'I swear, with you being away so often, I sometimes think you're having an affair.' She'd laughed it off, but Lucas was left feeling vulnerable.

He frequently felt overwhelmed, sure that it wasn't possible to keep the separate pieces of his life from colliding. His fear of being found out remained ever-present, along with a paranoia akin to the feeling of being tracked or hunted.

It all started as a bit of fun, a mechanism for coping with a loveless marriage. He thought it would help to eliminate the pain from the past if he constantly experienced that rush from a new love affair, but in actuality he suffered dismally at every turn and only succeeded in feeding his demons.

Occasionally, he tried to convince himself that the reason for his lifestyle—the infidelities—might be because, since losing Olivia, he'd been searching for true love in all the women he encountered, to recapture that evasive feeling. He hadn't found it again. It struck him as selfish, though, to try to justify his actions; his method of attempting to banish his heartache entailed cheating on numerous innocent women, as if eternally vengeful and determined to get even despite the blamelessness of his victims. His actions might have been a way of getting back at Olivia, but she was oblivious; it was like screaming into a void. If one of the women in his life discovered the dishonesty, there would be a domino effect, with waves of treachery flowing forward from the original one, transferring the pain to future generations.

'I went to your office today. You weren't there,' said Penny, hands on hips, accusing, when Lucas walked in through the door at 7 p.m. that evening.

'Um...' Heat rose in his cheeks. 'You must have missed me. Was it lunchtime? Or I might have popped out for a coffee.'

'They'd never even heard of you.'

'W-what were you doing there?' He hoped she'd stop talking.

'I wanted to have a chat with your boss about your ridiculous working hours.'

'I'm not a child. Do you know how embarrassing it would've been if—'

'You should've asked for time off; I was only trying to do what you should have done.'

'I don't work there anymore, okay?'

'What? When did you leave?'

'I haven't worked there for ages. I didn't tell you because I was looking for another job. I didn't want you to worry.'

'So you're unemployed?'

'No, I'm working for a company in the city. They're busy. I can't ask for a holiday when I only started working there last month. I don't want to lose the job. It was hard to find.'

'Why didn't you tell me?'

'I said. I didn't want you to worry.'

'Always thinking of others.' She softened. 'That's why I love you so much.'

Lucas breathed a sigh of relief.

'It must have been so hard for you to keep it a secret.'

'You have no idea,' he said.

◦❥◦

In the end, Lucas spent Christmas with Sally and the children. Luckily for him, Sally arranged to take Peter and Julie to her parents' house for the New Year period when he'd told her he had to work.

The New Year trip to Paris with Elayna surpassed his expectations. Paris was a gloriously romantic city: whether due to the ambience or just because it had always been portrayed as such in literature and in the movies, he couldn't be sure. The romance in the air around them, and Elayna's effervescent charm, brought out the inner vitality within his soul. He'd even found time to spend a passionate night with Delphine, slipping out of the hotel room for a few hours while Elayna slept.

Being away from London meant he saw things more clearly. The endless hiding, lying, cheating, and deceiving, fostered a state of perpetual anxiety. He saw that now. He contemplated staying in Paris. Having only two women in his life would be easier to manage.

He knew he would miss the others, though. Somehow he'd got used to the chaotic routine and mostly thrived on it. Like any addiction, it would be hard to give up.

Lucas and Elayna shared a pleasant flight back to London. He told her he'd have to leave her at Heathrow Airport so that he could go straight to work.

They stood outside the arrivals building and shared a lingering kiss before Elayna stepped into a taxi.

It took him a moment, after she'd departed, to work out where he should be going from there. Should he be headed home to Penny, or to Sally?

Just then, his mobile rang and he saw Penny's name on the display.

'Hello, love.'

'Hi Lucas, how are you?'

An odd question, he thought. They'd been married for so many years; they never asked each other *how are you?* It sounded more like something a stranger or acquaintance would ask. Perhaps it was her tone —the way she'd asked it—that caused the unease. 'Um... I'm okay.'

'Meet me inside the Terminal building. I'm in the Costa coffee shop.'

'The... Why?'

'I didn't know you were working abroad. I found your flight details and boarding pass in the bin, and realised you must've accidentally printed more than you needed.'

'Y-yes... I forgot about that. Sorry, yes, I was working abroad. A last-minute thing.'

But if she's seen my tickets, wouldn't she have seen Elayna's? I'm sure I threw them both in there.

Trepidatiously, he walked back into the airport building, mulling over the options available to him: *I'll say Elayna's my secretary.*

He felt foolish for throwing the ticket information into the bin at home. Recently, as his life became more perplexing, he'd found himself cutting corners. Suitcase in tow, he strolled towards the coffee shop. He stopped at the doors as if paralysed. *This can't be happening; I must be dreaming.*

Lucas blinked in a vain attempt to eliminate reality, prove it was just a dream. On opening his eyes, however, he was faced with the unimaginable again. He began to feel quite queasy. The chatter in the terminal around him sounded suddenly louder to his ears as panic took hold. Beads of sweat formed on his brow. He wondered if he might be suffering from delirium: seated around a table in the shop were Penny, Sally, and Loulla.

Penny waved.

Too late to run.

He walked slowly towards the table as a man to his death at the gallows.

'So, how long has this been going on?' asked Sally.

Lucas gulped. 'I'm sorry.'

All three women laughed.

'Sorry?' said Penny. 'You will be.'

'How... How did you...?' he gawped as the words escaped his mouth.

'We've known for a while,' said Sally. 'You thought you were so clever, didn't you? You left far too many clues. Mainly text messages and phone calls. You should've been more careful. You left your phone lying around.'

'And the boarding pass was the final straw,' said Penny.

'D-does Elayna know?' He thought back over the holiday in Paris; she'd given no indication that she might be aware of his duplicity, but everything was fuzzy in his recollection. He felt light-headed.

'She didn't, but she does now. I've just phoned her,' said Sally.

'You did what?'

'You should be ashamed of yourself,' snapped Loulla.

Dejected, he slumped down into the empty chair at the table. 'I am... I am. I don't know what to say.'

'Just go!' said Penny.

The abruptness of her command startled him.

'We've all decided that we don't want anything more to do with you,' said Sally.

'But the children—'

'They're better off without you,' sneered Penny.

'Yes,' agreed Sally. 'What kind of a role model are you?'

'Where will I go?'

'Who cares?' snorted Loulla.

'Goodbye, Lucas,' said Penny.

All eyes were on him, willing him to stand up and leave.

He eventually rose from the chair and dragged his suitcase away from the table. As he walked away, he looked over his shoulder in disbelief; the three women sat chatting over coffee, like old friends, as if he didn't exist.

He tried to recall how it had all started. Undoubtedly, the seed was planted by Olivia's unfaithfulness. In an attempt to forget her, he'd plunged into a new relationship, with Penny, and ended up married, almost without really knowing how, but ultimately the lottery win offered him the chance to alter the monotonous path his life had taken since.

After winning the jackpot on the lottery, he'd bought the house that he now lived in with Penny, pretending that the money came from his salary, lying about having a lucrative career. He'd splashed out on exotic holidays for her and the children, and lavish gifts for them. Then he'd met Loulla.

The thrill of having an affair went to his head. He liked the idea of being a James Bond type character, dating many women simultaneously. His wealth offered the freedom to turn his dreams into reality. For the first time in a long time, he woke up each morning without feeling the dread of humiliation that followed Olivia's betrayal, without thinking of what he'd lost.

He'd met Sally next. He hadn't intended them to have children together but it all spiralled out of control.

Starting from the enviable position of having too much time on his hands, he'd ended up with too many obligations.

Although the constant demands were hard to handle, a large black hole now opened up, occupying the space where his life had once been. He struggled to ignore the persistent dark thoughts telling him he might never see his children again. *I'll go and see a solicitor. I must have some rights...*

As he made his way to the Underground, he noticed a man lying outside a coffee shop in a sleeping bag. In the past, he'd wondered how people ended up like that, ashamed of himself at times for being so accustomed to ignoring their plight, often not even noticing them. This man's fate and his own now seemed infinitely more relatable. *I'm homeless*: the notion caused his heart to skip a beat. He couldn't go to the house he'd shared with Penny, not for the foreseeable future. Catching his breath, he reassured himself that there was a reasonable amount of money left from the lottery win, so he could stay at a hotel until he worked out what to do next. The money wouldn't last forever, though.

Anxiety took hold and he began to worry about the money running out. His frazzled brain raced ahead into the future and he pictured an old man, who looked a bit too familiar, his mirror image, sleeping on a park bench. He tried to focus on other things but his thoughts wandered to Olivia—they invariably did when anything in his life went wrong, as if an eternal circular pathway perpetually led back to her. Did she marry the man, the man with the face that frequently appeared in wishy-washy black and white flashbacks in Lucas's mind? Were they still living together, happily, while his own life fell to pieces?

As that thought mocked him, it was thankfully eclipsed by a more positive one: he remembered Debbie, the single mother he'd met at the park. The idea of her reached out to him like a beacon. *I'll go to the park tomorrow... Maybe she'll be there. I'll have to think of a reason why I haven't got the kids with me... Hmm... I'll take her up on her offer of a date. We'll visit Paris together —it was great seeing Delphine again...*

Where Do We Go?

The crowded room magnified Judy's sense of loneliness. Edward had waved at her when she arrived but then disappeared into the horde. Half an hour later, she sat alone with a deflated ego. Edward was at the bar, chatting to a blonde dressed as a vampire.

Judy shrugged away a twinge of jealousy, hating herself for caring. The story was old: a repetitive cycle. Unrequited love, like an addiction, whittled away the last remnants of self-esteem, little by little, every time she fell and every time she lost.

Stroking the velvet skirt of her dress, as if for comfort, Judy contemplated what to do next. She'd worn the dress to impress Edward; slinky, black, with a plunging neckline, it had been labelled "Temptress Witch" in the fancy-dress shop.

In the past half an hour, the room had become devoid of air. The place Edward had chosen for his Halloween party was far too small for the amount of people he'd invited. Judy estimated there might be about eighty people crammed in the stuffy venue. The music was too loud, causing everyone to shout instead of talk to each other, and the guests had to navigate their way through a throng every time they wanted to go to the bar or the toilet. Everyone appeared to be frowning, such was the ambience. Judy had arrived when it was a little less crowded and found a comfortable sofa at the back of the venue, but now there were people standing so close to her that she could feel the heat emanating from their bodies. It felt like sitting on a Tube train, except darker and even louder.

As she sat surrounded by people dressed as ghosts and ghouls, she was reminded of times when her older brother, Bill, used to hide and then unexpectedly leap out in front of her wearing scary costumes at this time of year. No matter how many times he did it, she never got used to it. It had left her with a nervous disposition.

A girl dressed as a zombie, who was standing beside the sofa, moved aside to let somebody by. Judy glimpsed Edward through the gap for a microsecond; he and the blonde vampire were laughing. Dejection raised its head as Judy thought of all the other times she'd believed she'd found *the one* only to be cast aside, overlooked, made to feel invisible.

She thought about leaving the party, no longer in the mood to socialise. Self-destructive thoughts abounded. As she sat alone on the sofa in the corner of the room, her illusions—or *delusions*—began to splinter.

A man with a horrific *Scream Ghostface* mask squeezed himself through the gap between a couple dressed as skeletons and sat down beside her on the sofa. He didn't say anything. Judy couldn't see his eyes properly because of the mask but assumed he was looking at her. She coughed in an attempt to break the silence. He didn't react.

Unnerved, she said, 'H-hello.'

'You mean you can see me?'

His voice sounded very deep, and distorted—almost as though it was computer-generated. Judy wondered if perhaps the mask could be causing the strange effect. 'Of course I can see you,' she replied, feeling disconcerted.

'Wow,' he said. 'I didn't realise anyone could; I'm usually invisible to the living. I was just joining in with the fun here. Gets lonely being undead, you know.'

'Undead?' Judy wished he would remove the mask.

The girl wearing the zombie costume smiled at her. Judy nodded and smiled back, embarrassed that the girl might have thought she was referring to her.

The strange man's voice thankfully came to the rescue: 'Yes, I'm dead. But I've been forced to wander the earth forevermore. I can't find my way to Heaven or Hell, not sure if they even exist. Not actually sure what I'm supposed to be doing. Well, I know that one of my jobs is to collect other undeads and initiate them... welcome them to their eternal misery. But you're not even dead, so I'm not sure how I'm able to communicate with you.'

'You're dead?' Judy wondered how strong the wine was that she'd been drinking. Although anxiety still hovered close by, she decided to play along with this man—if only to have something to focus on; the denseness of the atmosphere induced a sense of claustrophobia. 'How did you die?'

The zombie-girl laughed. 'How much have you had to drink, love?'

'It was a car accident,' said the man, distracting Judy. 'My own fault. I'd been drinking all night. I was already banned from driving at the time.'

'Oh.'

'She must be on something,' said the zombie girl to the couple dressed as skeletons.

Judy felt bemused as she watched the trio move backwards into the crowd as if to get away from her.

'That's a great costume you're wearing, Judy.' The deep voice of the creepy man sitting on the sofa distracted her.

'Thanks. Er... how did you know my name?'

'It's an undead thing. I kind of just know people's names, not sure how. It's like I have a higher knowledge but don't know how to use it.' He shrugged. 'Are we anywhere near Scotland?'

'Um... no, we're in London.'

'I occasionally end up in the wrong place. I'm supposed to be collecting an unfortunate soul from Scotland. I sometimes find myself in a place that has significance for the person I'm collecting. Maybe he or she was born here. Who knows? Could be they're not dead yet. I think I kind of tap into the person's mind for a while before they die and then it's easier to locate them. This one's leading me on a wild goose chase, though.'

Judy had tuned out of the conversation, still baffled as to how he knew her name. Did she introduce herself? She couldn't recall doing so. Could he have slipped a drug into her wine?

The *Ghostface-man* took off his mask and frowned. 'Sorry to have spooked you.'

His voice still sounded unusual, even without the mask; almost artificial. Forcing a smile, Judy said, 'Er... that's a great costume and I love your act. You almost fooled me.'

'Uh... Thanks,' said a man dressed as a vampire when Judy caught his eye. There was something like fear in his voice when he said it.

'Er... no, I was talking to him,' she said, turning and pointing to the man seated beside her. When she looked back she saw that the vampire man had found a gap in the crowd and made a quick exit, without even acknowledging her.

Perplexed, Judy turned to *Ghostface* and asked, 'Is anything wrong with my face? Has my make-up run, or something?'

'No, why?'

'Everyone's avoiding me. Maybe I'm just being paranoid.' She shrugged. 'Anyway, what was I saying? Yeah, I just said I like your act. It's good. But maybe you should drop it now and just be you.'

'Hmm... well, we have to find ways to pass the time, don't we?' *Ghostface-man* said. 'My name's Hendrix.'

'Cool name.'

'Yes, I chose it when I died. My actual name when I was alive was pretty boring.'

'Right, so you're back to being dead.' Judy sighed. 'What was your name when you were alive?'

'Mark.'

'I'm Judy.'

'Yes, I already know that.'

'Oh, yeah. But I still don't remember telling you my name.'

Judy couldn't help noticing that, despite there being hardly any room to move, the immediate area around the sofa was now clear of party-goers. Looking back at her companion, she wondered whether perhaps it might be Hendrix they were wary of. That would make sense.

His voice sounded so weird, and quite spooky, now that she thought about it.

'You must have told me your name when we first met,' said Hendrix. 'Or, as I say, I sometimes just know, especially when I'm getting information from the undead I'm collecting.'

'How do you make your voice sound like that?'

'It's the fire damage that did it. I used to have a great voice; I was a singer, you know. Only in my spare time, but our band was destined for greatness, I just know it. People used to compare my singing to Robert Plant.'

'You're determined to keep up this role-play, aren't you?' Judy giggled but more from nerves than amusement.

Hendrix narrowed his eyes before saying, 'Not sure what I'm doing at a Halloween party; parties were never really my thing even when I was alive.' He paused, then said, 'You don't like parties much either, do you?'

'Is it that obvious?'

'It is to me, but I know things.'

'Oh, yeah, you're an all-seeing undead person,' Judy stated wryly.

'You came alone.'

'Doesn't take a rocket scientist to work that out as I'm sitting on my own.'

'Edward invited you.'

'Um... it's his party, so again you wouldn't need a degree to be able to work that out.'

'How do you know Edward?'

'You tell *me*, since you know everything.'

'I didn't say I know everything. I just know some things. He broke your heart.'

Judy's cheeks reddened. 'H-how did... I mean, no he didn't. We're just Facebook friends.' As mortification descended, Judy now began to wonder about Hendrix. Was he a mind reader? A clairvoyant? There was no way he could have known about her infatuation. Was it that easy to tell that she had feelings for Edward? Then she wondered whether Edward had told him to speak to her; perhaps Hendrix had been looking to meet a single woman: *'Go and chat Judy up; she's desperate—always flirting with me on Facebook'.* That would explain how he knew her name.

'Who are you?' she blurted.

'I'm a Facebook friend of his too.'

It suddenly occurred to Judy that Edward's friends on Facebook would be able to see her comments on his posts and perhaps Hendrix had worked out that she fancied him. She turned towards where Edward sat at the bar and noticed that he seemed to be getting quite cosy with the

43

blonde, whispering into the woman's ear. Jealousy took hold again.

'He's a scientist,' said Hendrix.

'Yes,' she replied glumly. 'I don't know him very well.' *I don't know him very well.* She heard the words echo mockingly. Once again, she felt foolish for allowing herself to get carried away imagining that there could be anything between them. She'd met Edward twice, and even then it was only for a quick drink.

'I went to uni with him,' said Hendrix.

He wasn't looking at Judy, and he spoke whimsically as if remembering a fantastical bygone era, nostalgia colouring his words, telling of times he had spent with Edward and how everyone just knew he would become a scientist. The way he spoke about Edward, making him out to be a nice, ordinary guy, made Judy feel worse somehow.

'That's his latest girlfriend,' said Hendrix, pointing at the couple. 'Deborah. They've been seeing each other for a few weeks. It still surprises me how much I know about people by just looking at them. I wish I'd had that ability when I was alive, it would have saved me a lot of trouble.'

Girlfriend? How did I not know about that? Rejection and envy battled for the uppermost sensory position in Judy's mind. She contemplated what her life had become: an endless series of obsessions. Heartache and feelings of inadequacy were common companions; she felt stuck in a pattern that had become more of a prison.

She remembered reading somewhere a quote about why people always want what they can't have: it said that people frequently *ask* for failure so that when everything goes wrong they can feel, really *feel* something.

Whenever Judy was rejected she often ended up thinking it a fool's game to search for true love when there were a million alternatives, and wished that she didn't fall so quickly and so deeply for the wrong type of man, waiting, and wasting time and love.

Relationships were easy to come by and disposable, allowing an illusion of freedom. No one wanted to waste their time waiting for the real thing and developing spiritually, with all the darkness and solitude that entailed.

In her own fruitless search, over the years Judy had taken solace in literature: as chronicled in innumerable books and articles—fiction and non-fiction—by the greatest and most revered writers, century after century, the harsh reality seemed to be that no one ever found what they were looking for. Humans would only ever experience glimpses of what real happiness could be, mostly because it was hard to wait for any length of time under the pressure to conform. Conformity, with its tepid rewards, made people feel as if they belonged to something bigger than themselves, and everyone wanted to believe they belonged somewhere. Love—the one thing that could stop the endless search, the endless hopelessness—fell by the wayside, regarded as a dream for the foolish or the deluded.

Dave Gahan's voice synchronistically boomed over the speakers, the haunting closing lines of Depeche Mode's *"Going Backwards"* echoed her thoughts as the song came to an end.

Pushing away the negative feeling Judy forced a smile at Hendrix. 'I'll be leaving soon.'

'Oh, that's a pity. But yeah, I'll probably be off soon as well. As I say, parties aren't really my thing, and I'm miles from Scotland. I guess I'd better make my way up there.'

'It was nice to meet you,' said Judy, out of politeness.

'Yes, was nice to meet you too,' he replied. 'I think you're the only one who can see me, judging by the way people are looking at you. They think you're talking to yourself.'

Judy watched him walk away. The tremorous tone of his voice, and his words, had left a hollow sense of anguish in their wake—a black and dense, heavy burden, similar to the emotion she associated with mourning. It wouldn't disperse no matter how hard she tried to ignore it. *Maybe it was all the talk of death,* she mused; yet it was more than that.

She approached the bar and ordered a double whisky—not the most sensible solution, but she wanted to take the edge off the night's disappointment.

As she sipped her drink, she spotted Edward and Deborah sharing a kiss. She ordered another whisky. Lost in regret and humiliation, she heard someone call out, 'Judy!'. Looking up, she saw Edward waving from across the bar. She waved back and faked a smile. The next thing she knew, he was standing beside her.

'Glad you could make it, Judy,' he said, as if they were the best of friends. 'Love the costume.'

'Thanks.'

'You having a good time?'

'Er... yeah. I just met your friend, Hendrix.'

Edward squinted and it appeared he hadn't heard what she'd said. He smiled and shrugged. 'Sorry, it's too loud in here!' he remarked, leaning in towards her.

'I met Hendrix,' she said louder, into his ear.

He pulled away and nodded. 'Yeah, they should play some Hendrix. I'll ask the manager.'

Judy rolled her eyes.

Edward said something else that she didn't catch because of the loud music.

Judy watched as he returned to his seat, taking with him the ghosts of crossed wires and miscommunication that had haunted their relationship from the start.

Deborah pretended to suck blood from Edward's neck as he embraced her. Judy screamed inwardly. Deflated once again, she decided to leave.

When she stood up, the room appeared to spin and she had to remain still for a few moments before attempting to walk. She walked to the door on wobbly legs as the room continued to spin and sway and the noise of chatter and music boomed. Again, she worried about the possibility that Hendrix may have spiked her drink. Would he be waiting outside? Unable to shake the paranoia, she instinctively rubbed her arms where goosebumps had erupted.

As she exited the venue, the intro to *"All Along The Watchtower"* began to play. Frustration coloured her thoughts. The meeting with Edward played over and over in her mind like a bad movie: what she'd said; what she *should* have said; what he'd said; how he'd looked at her; what an idiot he must think she is. Overthinking, another burden to bear.

She put on her coat. The cool air was calming but she still found herself checking that Hendrix had gone. *'He broke your heart'*, his words came to mind. A tear threatened to fall as she conceded that it was the truth. She liked to think of herself as emotionally stable—idealistic but realistic—however, this deep wounded feeling wouldn't budge and she began to question her sanity.

On the way to the Tube station, she tried hard to focus on the now, knowing the past couldn't be changed. Just as she turned the corner of the street, someone jumped out in front of her wearing a terrifying zombie mask. 'Boo!' he shouted.

Judy fought with memories of her brother, cursing him for turning her into this nervous wreck.

The man removed his mask. 'Hi, Sis.'

'Bill?' She hadn't seen him for a few months; he lived in Manchester.

He hugged her tightly.

A smile spread across her lips and she felt instantly more relaxed as she asked, 'How come you're in London?'

'A friend's stag do with a Halloween theme.' He gestured to the zombie costume and raised his eyebrows.

They chatted for a while, catching up on family matters. His buoyant disposition was contagious and, soon, Judy found her dark mood dissipating.

A rowdy group of men exited the pub and one of them called out to Bill.

'I have to go,' said Bill, apologetically. 'It's a pub crawl so I'm guessing we're heading off to the next pub.'

'Okay, don't drink too much,' said Judy.

'Ha! You sound like Mum.' He laughed. 'Don't worry, I'm old enough and ugly enough to look after myself. You must visit soon, Sis. Isla and the kids would love to see you.'

'I've really missed you all. I'll try and visit soon.'

'It was great to see you. Take care of yourself.'

'You too.'

Bill ran over to join the rest of the group who were already walking away towards the Tube station. One of the men began singing a song that Judy had never heard before; the others joined in.

She couldn't help smiling as she watched them leave. Judy got home just after 11 p.m. and changed into pyjamas. Seeing Bill had cheered her up; all else was, for the moment, forgotten. Her mood changed when she found a missed call and a tearful voicemail message on her phone: 'Judy, it's Mum. Call me when you get this message, please.'

Feeling suddenly sober, Judy made the call and sighed with relief when her father answered the phone, having feared something might have happened to him.

'Dad? I had a message from Mum.'

'It's your brother,' was all he said.

'Bill?'

'He's been in an accident.'

'But... But I just saw him. About an hour ago. What happened?'

'You saw him? That's impossible. Where?'

'He was at a stag do in Camden.'

'Judy, you're getting confused. Your brother isn't in London. Listen, me and your mother will be visiting him in hospital tomorrow. We'll collect you on the way. He's in a coma; on life support. He's in a serious condition. All we know is that it was a car accident. We were told that he'd been drinking. It doesn't make sense; he was banned from driving. He mentioned it when your mother last spoke to him.'

Banned? Drinking? In the haze of Judy's mind, she recalled having a similar conversation with a man earlier in the evening.

'We're leaving quite early in the morning, about six o'clock. We don't want to be too late. Pack a bag, we'll stay with Isla overnight.'

'Too late? He's not going to...'

'Don't worry. Get some sleep. We don't know all the details yet.

47

Hopefully he'll be fine.'

Judy's head was spinning after the phone call. How could Bill have been in a car accident when his friends were all headed towards the Tube station? She was certain she'd seen him enter the station. Then she remembered what her father had said about drink-driving and her thoughts went to the party. Hendrix's nonsense story about him being undead was so similar. Perhaps she was imagining things. She tried to recall how many drinks she'd had.

Hendrix had said he was a Facebook friend of Edward's. She decided to look him up if only to prove to herself that she wasn't completely losing her mind. She found her laptop and logged on to Facebook. There was a message notification from Edward; he'd sent a message thanking everyone for attending the Halloween party. Judy checked the names included in the bulk message. No Hendrix. She scanned the list for a Mark, but there wasn't one.

She clicked through to Edward's Facebook page. He'd updated his status to "in a relationship" with Deborah Squires. She fought the overwhelming sense of rejection and searched through Edward's Friend list. Soon she found the man she'd been speaking to earlier: Mark Porter; recognising his face from the profile photo. Without thinking about it, she sent him a friend request.

After packing an overnight bag ready for the trip to see Bill at the hospital, she returned to the computer. There was a message notification on Facebook from Mark.

Hello. Thank you for the friend request. This page is being kept open as a memorial for Mark, who sadly passed away last Halloween. I can add you as a friend if you knew him but otherwise we'd like to keep it for friends and family only. I hope you understand. Mark's mother, Daisy.

Mark/Hendrix certainly had a warped sense of humour. Judy rolled her eyes and clicked through to his Facebook page. The blood washed from her face as she scrolled through hundreds of messages of condolence. *How can this be true?*

His words echoed in her mind: *You mean you can see me?... I'm dead... one of my jobs is to collect other undeads and initiate them... welcome them to their eternal misery...*

Judy covered her ears, in a futile attempt to block out the incessant inward chatter. With trembling hands, she replied to his mother's message: **I'm sorry for your loss. I had no idea Mark had died.**

This is all a dream. None of it can possibly be true. I'm losing my mind. It must be the whisky. I need to sleep.

A few hours later, Judy was awoken by the phone ringing. She reached over to the bedside cabinet to pick it up. 'Hello,' she said in a croaky voice.

'Darling, it's Mum. I'm so sorry to have to tell you this.' She began to cry.

'Mum? Is it Bill?'

'Yes. He... He didn't make it. The doctor said he was critical; we should have gone straight away.'

'Stop... There was nothing we could have done.'

'Isla and the children were at his bedside when— I'm so glad they got there in time to say goodbye; it was a bit of a trek for them from Manchester.'

A trek? So he was in London, after all... Judy wished she could rewind time, delete the past few hours, return to the night before and stop Bill from getting into his car. She blinked away tears.

'Are you all right, darling?' Her mother's voice cracked as she asked the question.

Judy tried to say yes, but she knew that if she spoke she would cry.

'Take your time. It must have come as a shock. We'll come and see you later, darling; maybe I shouldn't have told you over the phone.'

Judy recalled that after the conversation with her dad the night before—when he'd said that Bill wasn't in London—she'd been convinced that Mark must have spiked her drink, causing a hallucination when she thought she'd seen Bill. Thinking back to their meeting, she felt strangely comforted by that one last memory of her brother.

'He was so happy last night, enjoying himself with his friends. He said I should visit. Mum, why didn't I visit them more often? I took it for granted that he'd always be there. He was always there but now I'll never see him again.'

'Darling, don't upset yourself. No one could have guessed something like this would have happened.'

'It was so good to see him last night.'

'What? How? You couldn't have seen him last night.'

'Yes, I did. It was unexpected. He was in Camden. I bumped into him on my way home, well he jumped out at me dressed in a Zombie costume, remember like he used to do when we were kids? He said he was at a stag do.'

'You're getting confused, darling. It must be the grief. Bill was at a stag do, yes. But it was in Edinburgh.'

'Edinburgh? But—'

'Yes, his friend Phil is getting married. You remember Phil, don't you? You all used to play together when you were children. I have to go, love, your father isn't taking this very well. We'll come and see you later.'

One Chance

As Hilda stepped off the train, it caught her eye, gleaming like a star misplaced on land. She felt drawn to the gold pendant, as if an extrinsic force were compelling her to pick it up. It was shaped like an insect—not quite a beetle, more of a scorpion without the tail. Commuters hurried past, no one appeared to be searching for anything. The pendant seemed strange but familiar, as though she'd seen it before, but she knew she hadn't. More than that, it drew her to it like it was something that belonged to her. *Maybe I owned it in a former lifetime...* Hilda marvelled at the fantastical thought that entered her mind unexpectedly; this little piece of jewellery had certainly awakened her imagination.

She picked up the curiosity and placed it in her coat pocket. As she observed the steady stream of busy commuters fighting their way along the platform, her mind boggled as to how she'd spotted the tiny treasure amidst the throng. *Perhaps it found me.* Again she was surprised by her peculiar thought. The pendant appeared to possess a mystical quality; she recalled how the station platform had practically faded into the background when she'd first seen the pendant, her attention fixed on the tiny gold object, oblivious to everything else.

'Excuse me,' huffed a flustered middle-aged woman.

Hilda muttered 'Sorry,' up until then unaware that she had been blocking an exit, caught up in obsessing over the trinket she'd found, lost in a place out of time.

As unlikely as it may seem, when Hilda arrived home all thoughts of the mysterious pendant were superseded by other more mundane musings, such as what she would cook for dinner.

She walked towards her front door and heard the neighbour's gate creak open.

'Hello, dear. Could you help me carry my shopping into the house? This trolley's quite heavy and I always struggle to lift it over the threshold.'

'No problem, of course,' replied Hilda.

Hilda often helped Florrie, a woman in her seventies, who had lived alone since her husband died the year before. Florrie was in good health but did suffer from arthritis, especially at this time of year.

'How are you today, Florrie?'

'Fine, thanks dear. Mustn't grumble. My daughter came to visit with my grandson, Charlie. I love that boy, but he has so much energy and always makes such a mess of the house, throwing toys here and there.' The older woman giggled and rolled her eyes.

Hilda helped Florrie with her shopping, and tidying up. As she leaned over to put a toy car into a basket, the scorpion pendant fell from her pocket and clattered onto the wooden floor. Hilda picked it up.

'Oh, what's that, dear?'

She turned to Florrie, red-faced. 'It's just a pendant; I found it on the Tube platform on my way home from work. It was too pretty to leave it there. Do you think maybe I should have left it, in case the owner was looking for it?'

'Let me see,' said Florrie.

Hilda held out her hand to reveal the pendant.

Florrie took two steps backwards and put a hand over her mouth.

'W-what's wrong?' asked Hilda.

'It can't be,' said Florrie, almost inaudibly.

'Is it yours?' asked Hilda, with a confused frown.

'No. No, it's Edna's.'

'Who's Edna?'

'She... Oh, no, never mind. It can't be hers.' Florrie turned around and headed for the front door. 'I expect you've got things to do, Hilda. Thank you for helping with the shopping and the cleaning.'

Hilda tried to ask another question but Florrie opened the door and said, 'Sorry, dear, I feel a migraine coming on. You'll have to leave.'

After her unceremonious expulsion, Hilda stood outside and stared at her neighbour's closed front door for a while. Florrie obviously recognised the pendant. Or perhaps the pendant brought back unpleasant memories of the past. And who was Edna? Hilda wanted to knock on the door, desperate for some kind of answer, some way to make sense of Florrie's bizarre behaviour. Instead, she went back to her own house. A few moments later, she found herself seated on the sofa unable to recall walking to it or sitting down, her mind abuzz with questions. Slowly, she unclenched her fist and looked at the curious scorpion-shaped pendant. *I should've left it on the platform.* The longer she stared at it, however, the more she warmed to it. It was beautiful, shining, seemingly reflecting invisible lights, lights that couldn't be seen by the human eye. She smiled, as she had done on first discovering the pendant; it had quite an uplifting effect. *I wonder if it's magical,* the thought fluttered through Hilda's mind and, as it did so, the trinket fell unexpectedly to the floor. Catching her breath, Hilda leaned over to pick it up, her heart beating faster than normal. She wondered aloud: 'What are you?' *It might be possessed.* A shiver followed the thought, along with an image in her head of a commuter jumping from the Tube platform to certain death, the scorpion pendant falling to the ground.

The doorbell rang, providing a welcome distraction.

Hilda caught her breath and placed the pendant on the coffee table before rising from the sofa to answer the door.

Florrie stood outside, wearing a frown. 'Hello, dear. Can I come in?'

'Of course.' Hilda stood to one side to allow the woman to enter. Only then did she see that Florrie was holding what appeared to be an old photo album.

Florrie went into the living room and sat on the sofa.

Hilda noticed that her eyes were fixed upon the gold pendant on the table. The woman's hand clutched at the arm of the sofa, as if for reassurance.

Hilda sat next to her. 'Are you all right?'

Florrie stared at the pendant for a few more seconds before appearing to awaken from a trance. 'I'm so sorry about earlier,' she explained, 'I was just surprised to see... I never expected to ever see the scorpionite pendant again.'

'Scorpionite?'

'It's almost genetically identical to a scorpion. It has a magnet. Not the kind of magnet you have here. It doesn't exist on planet Earth. It's a magnet that attracts hearts.'

Hilda giggled. 'Doesn't exist on planet Earth? An alien scorpion then?'

Florrie let out a breath, and then said, 'What I'm going to tell you is a secret. I've never told anyone. I believe I can trust you because Edna has chosen you.'

'Chosen me...? For what? Who's Edna?' Hilda stared blankly at Florrie.

'Before Edna left Earth she told me she would choose our successor. I don't have long in this world. I'll be returning home to Meitera soon and I need a successor, I just never thought it would happen so soon. You see, the pendant is a sign, it's the calling.'

Hilda began to worry about Florrie's mental health. Her grandson's visit must have scrambled her brain. 'Are you feeling all right, Florrie? Shall I call your daughter?'

'I know it sounds ridiculous, fantastical, unbelievable, and well, I suppose it is all of those things, but it's true. I'm from a different planet. My home planet is called Meitera. It hasn't been discovered by Earthlings yet, but we've known about your planet for millions of years. Our technology is far more advanced. There are hundreds of us on planet Earth and we live here in human bodies and report back to our planet. Every five years we recruit Earthlings to take over our role and become one with us. The idea is to take as many Earthlings with us to Meitera as we can because Earth is becoming unstable, life is uncertain, and humans are imperfect and mortal. We only take the best Earthlings, so you should feel flattered to have been chosen. We wouldn't take anyone with the propensity for crime or who is the type to judge others. On Meitera we respect all citizens and we live forever. Death only occurs if a Meiterian commits a crime against a fellow citizen, then death is instant. It's rare.'

'You're an alien?'

'I prefer the term *visitor*. On Earth you depict aliens as ugly and most often green. I am none of those things. Meiterians are made of light. My natural form is more like what you'd imagine an angel to look like, but without wings.'

Hilda began to laugh. Just a giggle at first but then it became uncontrollable, involuntary. Quivering with nervous energy, she tried to stop herself laughing. 'I'm sorry,' she spluttered between giggles.

'The funny thing is,' said Florrie, seemingly oblivious to Hilda's fit of laughter, 'I was rather enjoying my time here. I'd almost fooled myself that I could stay for as long as I wished, but it doesn't work that way. I'm being called back now. I must leave you in charge.'

'Right,' said Hilda, knitting her brow. 'Thank you, Florrie. I'm honoured to have been chosen, really, but I'm a bit busy now, so let's talk about this another time.' She stood up and walked towards the living room door.

'There is no time, Hilda. If I don't pass on the knowledge to you now, it will be too late. Edna will not hesitate to choose another successor. You only get one chance.'

Hilda approached the front door and opened it. Florrie still cradled the photo album, which sparked Hilda's curiosity, but it wasn't enough to chase away the urgent desire to get her neighbour out of the house.

'I'm sorry, Florrie. I don't want to go to Meitera.' A wrinkle of concern formed on her brow.

'Very well. I'm sorry to have bothered you. We will leave you in peace.'

Hilda watched her leave, once again bemused by the woman's behaviour.

Aliens? Or visitors... Ha! Oh, my God, what is going on? I hope she's okay. Hilda shook her head, as if in an attempt to rid it of the memory of Florrie's visit. She headed straight to the kitchen and prepared her supper.

Later, as she placed a cup of tea on the coffee table, she noticed the scorpion pendant wasn't there. She checked underneath the table and even under the sofa. It had gone. *I bet Florrie took it.*

Had Florrie recognised the pendant as an antique and concocted her story as a means of getting access to it and stealing it? She'd never thought of Florrie as a dishonest woman, but her odd behaviour this evening left questions in Hilda's mind.

Hilda avoided Florrie for the next couple of weeks, leaving extra early for work and coming home later than usual.

One evening, she saw a "For Sale" sign in her neighbour's front garden. As she approached the gate, Florrie's daughter, Amy, exited the house.

'Hello,' said Hilda.

'Hi.' Amy smiled but appeared weary.

'I didn't know Florrie was selling.'

'Um... my mum...' Amy fiddled with her gloves as she tried to put them on with shaky hands.

Hilda saw the woman's eyes were full of tears.

'Mum died last week.' Amy wiped away a stray tear with her leather glove.

'I'm so sorry. I had no idea.'

Amy smiled sadly before walking away.

Hilda recalled Florrie's words: 'I *don't have long in this world.*' ... '*I'm being called back...*'

Don't be silly; she was an old woman. Old women die. She wasn't an alien...

Hilda went into her house, pondering the unusual events and whether she'd imagined them all.

৩৵৶

A few days later, Amy visited Hilda.

Hilda made her a cup of tea and they sat together in the living room. It made her sad to think of Florrie sitting in the same place her daughter now sat, a couple of weeks before.

'I can't stay long,' said Amy after taking a sip of tea. 'I only came because I know you were a friend of my mum's and I wanted to invite you to the funeral. It's going to be at St Mark's church, across the road, on Sunday. Amy reached into her handbag. 'Mum made a will. She wanted you to have this photo; it was taken in her schooldays. That's her, and that's her best friend, Edna. They remained good friends up until Edna died a few years ago. They were more like sisters, really. It's just an old photo, but I'm sure she must have had her reasons for wanting you to have it. It's nice; very antique-looking. You could frame it. Mum was beautiful when she was young. So was Edna.'

Hilda smiled as she took the photo from Amy. Taking a cursory glance, she remembered her conversation with Florrie. 'Amy, did your mother ever mention anything about Meitera to you?'

'Ha, ha! Planet Meitera? Yes, she always said she came from Meitera; said she was "visiting".' Amy laughed. 'I've heard the story a hundred times. So she told you too, hey?'

'Yes.'

'She had a wonderful imagination. As much as it used to drive me mad, I'll miss those old stories now. I truly will.' Amy had a faraway look in her eye. 'Oh well, we have the memories.'

The two women chatted for a while longer and then Amy left to collect her son from a friend's house.

Hilda sat alone when Amy had gone, wondering about Florrie. She picked up the photograph and couldn't help the smile that came to her lips. Although she'd not known Florrie as a young woman, there could be no doubt that the girl in the photo was her. Her eyes were unmistakable— striking and dark, they'd always shone full of hope and light. Even in this frayed black and white photograph, her eyes stood out, full of life, vibrant.

Florrie and Edna must have been about thirteen years old when the photo was taken. They wore joyful expressions; two young girls without a care in the world. Then Hilda noticed a pendant resting on Edna's blouse. The scorpion... or *scorpionite* pendant. 'It can't be,' said Hilda, echoing Florrie's reaction at being shown the pendant. *It's a coincidence*, thought Hilda. *There must be hundreds of those pendants. Someone lost it on the Tube, that's all.*

Hilda attended Florrie's funeral and laughed and cried at the family's speeches. The stories about Meitera were related by a couple of the family members during their speeches. It turned out that Edna also used to tell the tales. The girls had concocted the story of the undiscovered planet when they were schoolgirls, driving their families crazy with their storytelling over the years. It put a whole new perspective on everything for Hilda. She found it endearing, and came away from the funeral realising that Florrie was a fun person, the sort of woman to make up fanciful tales to entertain her family and friends. She felt much better after the funeral and ended up becoming good friends with Amy and her family for years to come.

56

Ten years later, Hilda sat watching the news when she heard her daughter crying over the baby monitor. She went upstairs to check on her daughter and missed the story at the end of the regional news:

"Scientists have discovered a distant planet similar to Earth. It is thought that the air quality could potentially sustain life. There are unconfirmed reports of intelligent life on the planet— although this is, as yet, unsubstantiated. It is thought the planet is millions of years old. Scientists have given it the name Meitera, with the nickname Sister Earth."

lex talionis

Oscar sat by his desk and looked out of the window. Beyond the vast garden, the seemingly never-ending expanse of ocean merged into the sky creating a beautiful backdrop. Looking out on the magnificent view made Oscar feel small and insignificant. It had long been a dream of his to live by the sea and somewhere away from the hustle and bustle. He'd achieved his goal, but something was missing. The loneliness had never been part of his dream. He didn't allow himself to think too deeply about it for fear of falling into regret. Whenever he allowed regret to penetrate his conscious thoughts, a darkness took over, consuming his days and nights, giving him no peace.

For forty long years Oscar worked a nine-to-five office job. The words of that Dolly Parton song occasionally made their way to his mind on the daily commute: he'd literally gone "crazy", he mused, and through no fault of his own. He blamed the life of rigid and dull routine for everything.

Everything.

How unnatural to expect someone to wake up to an alarm clock every day and rise before the sun, to get on a crowded train only to be abused by other frustrated commuters, and to work in an office for eight hours at a monotonous job before getting on another crowded train home. The tedium of the job itself, the competitiveness and power-play of colleagues and managers, as well as overwhelming demands from clients, drained his energy. Everything he did was for someone else's benefit, it seemed: his boss, the company that employed him, the clients—never for himself. After toiling for years, he didn't have much to show for it, as his wife had often reminded him.

Oscar always dreamed of retiring to the sea or to the countryside. He had the best of both here, but happiness eluded him. Ghosts and memories were his constant companions.

He turned his attention away from the window and back to his computer. After a lifetime of following orders, he could finally devote time to his passion: writing. Somehow, though, the words would not come. He'd believed writer's block was a concept made up by people who were not really writers but wanted to appear as if they were; he'd not suffered from this problem in the past. Usually, whenever he put pen to paper—or fingers to the keyboard—the words flowed, with hardly any effort on his part. However, since Hannah's death, the skill was lost to him. Perhaps she'd taken it with her.

As memories of Hannah entered his mind, black thoughts

encircled him. They'd often talked about a retirement where they could spend every day doing what they loved. It seemed like an unattainable dream. They'd been living in a cramped apartment getting on each other's nerves. Hannah couldn't work because of illness, and Oscar brought in just enough money to keep them both alive.

He'd promised her a better life when he retired, but that day always seemed so far away. The arguments were an everyday occurrence. He would snap at her when he felt stressed out, and she'd moan about being stuck indoors, complaining that he didn't do enough to help her. He'd question why Hannah couldn't find something to do, working from home, and she'd get offended and call him uncaring. It went around and around continually, until Oscar started to hate going home. He hated going to work and hated returning home. Life became unbearable.

He'd contemplated leaving Hannah, but every time the thought came to mind he felt bad. They'd been married for twenty-five years and for the first ten years they were happy. Hannah always cheered him up with her positive views on life. The illness changed everything, taking her over and turning her into a different person. Negativity pervaded her thoughts, words, and actions. He knew the illness wasn't her fault, wasn't her choosing. He wanted to blame her but couldn't. So, he started to blame his job. He'd find himself in a bad mood every morning when the alarm clock sounded.

Oscar began to yearn for what was lost: he wanted the old Hannah back. This imposter wasn't Hannah. He wasn't sure when it started, but the feeling refused to go away. A struggle in his mind constantly taunted him. If he left her, their friends and family would see him as the bad person. *In sickness and in health,* he had vowed, *Till death do us part.* He tried his best to infuriate her many times over the years, in an attempt to make her want to leave him—but his energy ran out. It was clear she wasn't going anywhere.

Hannah's last words to him were: 'All you think about is work, work, work.'

That's when he'd killed her.

No one knew.

They'd argued and he'd pushed her forcefully, wishing she'd disappear. Hannah hit her head on the edge of some wooden furniture.

She never woke up.

Oscar called an ambulance straight away and said it was an accident, she'd fallen; he explained that her illness affected her mobility. The hospital didn't question his version of events.

Friends and family were devastated. They showered him with love and brought him food, offering to help with chores.

'You were such a good husband, looking after her for so long. Don't blame yourself.'

He'd heard those words from more than one person: *Don't blame yourself*. Whenever he heard them, he felt a tug of guilt and a sense of paranoia: feeling sure everyone must be able to guess what he'd done. He'd killed her. He told himself he hadn't meant to do it, he had only pushed her—but he knew, when he'd pushed her he wanted her gone. His thoughts condemned him; if he hadn't pushed Hannah she'd still be alive.

The guilt ate away at his mind. An innocent man would have just explained to the paramedics that they'd argued and although he'd pushed her, he hadn't meant to hurt her. The question mark surrounding his culpability remained. In the months prior to her death he'd fantasised about somehow being rid of her. He didn't *plan* to kill her, but after her fall he'd not felt anything. It came as a relief. He wasn't shaken or shocked; on the contrary, he remembered thinking that he finally felt free.

Oscar glanced at the clock beside his desk before looking back at the view out of the window; it was a view that should have ignited his imagination but instead just reflected the blankness of his mind. He noticed the sun had begun its descent into the ocean—that's the way he saw it: the sun sank into the ocean overnight and then rose the next day from the waves. The sun setting indicated to Oscar that another day was over. He felt deflated, knowing he'd held such hope in the morning that this might be the day he would write his next great story. He'd written a few paragraphs in the morning and deleted them in the afternoon. It left him feeling that the magic no longer existed; whatever talent he'd possessed enabling him to write freely in the past was no more. He mused that it was probably the law of nature: if you did something wrong, hurt someone else, you'd suffer by losing your dearest passion. It made sense, but it was something he found hard to accept. In the three months since he'd moved into this place he'd only written one story, and he didn't think it was any good.

In the early days, Hannah had supported his writing efforts; she was his biggest fan. They'd even talked about how one day they'd be living in a house like this, purchased with his royalties. In the last ten years, however, her bitterness, like a fire extinguisher, put out any sparks of joy that might have arisen when he talked of his writing efforts.

'It's just a hobby, Oscar. Be realistic. You're never going to amount to anything. How many years have you been trying and failing? The definition of insanity is doing the same thing over and over again and expecting different results, you know.'

'Plenty of famous authors were self-published writers,' he would argue.

'Keep fooling yourself. It doesn't pay the rent. You need to concentrate on the job that does pay you a salary, maybe then you wouldn't be stuck in a dead-end job and might actually have made something of yourself.'

◈

A few months after Hannah's death, Oscar received unexpected news: his novel, one that had been rejected multiple times over the years, would be published by a well-respected large publishing house. This was after more than twenty years of his writing efforts coming to nothing. He felt elated and for a short time almost forgot his guilt about what happened to Hannah. He saw the publishing deal as a sign: Hannah forgave him, and from somewhere out there—wherever she'd gone—she had helped him secure this book deal.

He'd bought this property using the advance he received from the publishing house. When he moved in, he had one of Hannah's photographs enlarged and framed with a beautiful gold frame—it was a photo from the happier times, when she was still young and hopeful; hope exuded from her eyes in the photograph. It was one of his favourites.

The happy feeling didn't last. Most of the time he felt as if he was a lost soul stranded in the middle of nowhere. He'd signed a contract with the publishers and they were expecting more stories, stories that just wouldn't come.

As he stood up now and stretched his legs, he turned to face the photograph of Hannah on the wall. He was starting to see it differently, it only served to remind him that she was gone and he'd played his part in that. He walked towards it, making the decision to take it down. Reaching towards the top of the frame, he tripped on the edge of a rug, landed on the wooden floor and hit his head on the side of some furniture.

He never woke up.

Think Twice

Susan noticed the blue police tape on her way to the local shop to buy a loaf of bread. Immediately her thoughts went to recent stabbings and shootings in the area. Only the evening before she'd heard of a double-shooting in another London borough, and now it had happened again, not too far away from her own front door.

Tom was watching television when she walked into the living room.

'There's been another stabbing,' he said without taking his eyes from the screen.

'I know, I've just seen the police tape in Mottle Avenue,' she replied.

'A girl this time. Not sure it's even gang related.'

'Oh dear. How old?'

'In her twenties. Nice girl, from what her mum says. Went to university.' He stood up and shook his head. 'I'm going to make a cup of tea, you want one?'

'No, thanks.'

Susan felt sick to the stomach when she saw the evening news later that day.

Seeing Lorraine's face again in these circumstances was surreal. She remembered how she'd hoped she would never see her again after Lorraine left her office a few months ago. She also remembered thinking —whenever she was feeling exceptionally angry—that if she did see her again she would like to strangle her.

Lorraine had caused nothing but trouble when she'd worked with her a few months ago; the immature girl had sent an unfounded letter of grievance against her to HR, almost costing her the job she had worked so hard for. Susan had even thought to herself, at the time, that one day Lorraine would mess with the wrong person and perhaps meet a grizzly end. But as Lorraine's smiling face stared back at her from the TV screen —her graduation photo—something tugged at Susan's heartstrings.

The local newspaper covered the incident the following day:

Office Worker Left For Dead

Lorraine Pearson-Palmer, 23, had been working for

a temping agency and was stabbed after leaving her place of work at 4pm on Tuesday. Police are looking for witnesses to the brutal attack.

'She is such a beautiful clever girl,' her mother said, through tears, in a formal statement. 'Please find the monster who did this to my precious child. They could have killed her. Lorraine would never hurt anyone, I don't understand why someone has done this.'

Colleagues at her workplace were unavailable for comment.

Susan looked at the picture of Lorraine on the front page of the paper; the same graduation photo that had been on the TV. The idea that perhaps Lorraine had done something similar to what she had done to her, and then been punished by someone, had been going around in Susan's mind all night and for most of the day. She wanted to visit Lorraine, to talk to her and find out what had happened.

When she told Tom, he looked at her as if she'd lost her mind. 'Hang on a minute, you told me this is the girl who nearly lost you your job with her lies, and now you want to visit her in hospital?'

'I know it sounds stupid.'

'You hated her.'

'I did. And, you know, it's been a few months since it happened and sometimes I still think of her and have hateful thoughts. But maybe if I visit her and find out what happened, maybe I can help her.'

'Help her? You're too soft. She deserved to die. Pity she survived. Do you remember what a state you were in when you had to go through the disciplinary procedure at work and you thought you'd lose your job? Your hair started falling out, remember?'

'I know, but I didn't lose my job.'

'What good would come of you visiting her?'

'I could make her understand that her behaviour could have led to this stabbing. Maybe she doesn't even know the danger that she's putting herself in. She's young, immature. You saw how much hate and anger I had towards her. If I'd been a violent person, I probably would have tried to kill her.'

'People like that deserve everything they get.'

'I used to think like that, but I don't anymore. In a roundabout way, Lorraine has made me change the way I think about these things. I

63

wanted something bad to happen to her, I really did, but when I heard this news... It's so important that we forgive each other, otherwise we're just as bad as the person with the knife.'

'You're too nice, Susan. That's your problem. That's why people like Lorraine take advantage of you.'

On Monday, Susan's boss, Jemima, told everyone at the office that she'd been in touch with Lorraine's mother and was hoping to collect some money to buy a gift and a card for Lorraine to cheer her up, as she knew she was feeling quite low after the stabbing.

'I think it would be nice if we all contributed and maybe even if some of us visited her at hospital,' said Jemima. 'Her mother says she's going to be kept there for a couple of weeks.'

❧

Susan had offered to deliver the gift and card to Lorraine on behalf of her colleagues.

She hesitated as the bus stopped outside the hospital. She wasn't sure she could go through with seeing her again. Wouldn't it just stir up old painful memories? For months after Lorraine left the office, Susan had tried to work out in her mind why Lorraine had stooped so low and made the complaint against her. As far as Susan was concerned she had only ever been nice to Lorraine, and it had made her feel terrible and physically sick when she'd received the letter Lorraine had sent to HR making Susan out to be a bully.

She stepped off the bus at the last minute, just before it was going to pull away. Taking a deep breath she tried to blank out the negative thoughts from her mind. Would Lorraine even agree to see her?

A few minutes later, Susan was seated in the waiting area having been told that Lorraine was having some routine tests and she would be able to see her after the doctor had left.

'Ms Cartwright?'

Susan stood up when she heard the nurse call her name. She walked over to the door and was led to Lorraine's ward.

After the nurse left her, Susan slowly made her way over to Lorraine's bed, her mind deluged with unwanted thoughts. How would Lorraine greet her? Would she somehow think Susan was happy that she was here? Would she think Susan was being insincere?

Lorraine's mouth fell open when she saw Susan.

Susan instinctively smiled, 'Lorraine, how are you feeling?' Was that the right thing to ask, would it come across as sarcastic? The thoughts

64

continued to give Susan no peace.

Lorraine looked down at the sheet covering her legs and closed her eyes briefly. 'What are you doing here?' she said with a blank expression on her face, which Susan couldn't read.

'I-I came to bring you a card and gift.' Susan found she was speaking quickly, 'We had a collection for you at the office. Everyone was shocked to hear what had happened to you.'

'Even you?' asked Lorraine.

Susan smiled. 'Yes. Yes, even me. I know the way you left was... Well. Look, the past is the past, water under the bridge. I've forgiven you.'

Lorraine shot a look at Susan. 'Forgiven me? You have some nerve. Didn't you even read the letter I sent to HR?'

'I read it,' said Susan, lowering her eyes. 'It was hurtful. I have no idea why you wrote it, but that's part of the reason I'm here today, actually.'

Lorraine looked at her with wide eyes. 'I bet you were the one who told someone to stab me, weren't you? Oh, my God. Get out of here. I'm going to tell the police.'

'Lorraine, you have to stop making false accusations against people. That's probably why you were stabbed. I didn't have anything to do with it, but think about it, have you made any other false claims against someone, someone who might have got so angry that they wanted you dead?'

'I don't have to listen to you!' screeched Lorraine. 'For all I know you set up the stabbing and now you're trying to make out that you like me, bringing me this gift and card so that the police won't find out.'

'I'm going to go now,' said Susan, 'but think about what I said. You could have died. Everyone's worried about you; your mum, everyone at work. Even me. When I heard the news about what had happened it made me sad. I just wanted a chance to talk to you and try to make you understand that the way you behave—'

'You're not my mum. You don't have a right to tell me how to behave. Go away, I don't want you here.' Lorraine pressed the bell behind her bed.

Susan shook her head and walked away wondering why she had even tried. Lorraine was never going to change.

As Susan made her way home she felt her anxiety levels rise. What if Lorraine told the police that she thought she had something to do with the stabbing? She tried to block out the thoughts, knowing it was ridiculous; she'd been at work when the stabbing took place. But what if Lorraine concocted a story to say that Susan had been behind the stabbing, had arranged it? By the time she got home, Susan was a quivering wreck. She fell into Tom's arms and cried for a few minutes before she was able to speak and tell him what had happened.

'I told you, didn't I? I don't know why you went to see that no good pathetic loser. Anyway, don't concern yourself. Someone has been arrested for the stabbing. Her ex-boyfriend apparently. He was caught on CCTV. It was on the news while you were out.'

'Are you sure?'

'Yes.'

Susan breathed a sign of relief and sat down on the sofa, only then realising that she was still holding the carrier bag which contained Lorraine's gift; expensive chocolates and a nice bracelet. She tore open the wrapping paper and put the bracelet on. Then she opened the chocolates and offered one to Tom. While he told her about his day, she tore the card that the staff had signed for Lorraine into small pieces and threw it into the waste paper bin by the side of the sofa.

Leaning back she took a couple of the chocolates, delighting in the way they melted on her tongue, feeling happy she would never see Lorraine again.

Ain't That Peculiar

The full moon appeared to be shining a spotlight on the garden, as if conspiring against him. Ross cursed under his breath. There were only a few hours until dawn, he had to think quickly.

This was the third time he'd killed a man. He would continue to do it for as long as was necessary. Tatiana wasn't a bad person, it was these men; they were the ones to blame.

He recalled how betrayed he had felt when he found out about Joel. He'd found a text message on Tatiana's phone one night, two years ago.

Thank you for a lovely evening. We must do it again soon. Love Joel x

He'd asked Tatiana about it, and she'd told him Joel was her cousin from out of town, they'd met up after not seeing each other for a few years and had gone to dinner. She often went out to dinner with Joel after that, never inviting Ross to join them. 'I'm meeting Joel' would become a common response whenever Ross suggested they should go out.

He found out that Joel wasn't really Tatiana's cousin a few months later when he'd returned from a business trip one day earlier than expected and discovered him in the bathroom getting dressed.

'Who are you?' Ross had asked.

'I'm Joel. Who are you?'

Tatiana had not heard Ross arrive and walked into the bathroom after him, naked. Ross turned around and saw the shock on her face as she registered what was happening.

'This is your cousin?' Ross had said.

Tatiana began to cry and ran out of the room.

'Tatty, who is this man?' Joel had asked, following her out of the bathroom.

Ross watched as Joel embraced Tatiana.

'I'm going to ask you one question,' Ross said, stepping into the hallway, trying to keep his composure. 'Is this your cousin?'

'Sorry, Ross,' she'd said. 'I've been lying to you, but you must know our relationship is over. I'm dating Joel.'

Joel never responded to any of Tatiana's calls after that. Only Ross knew why. He'd stayed at the flat, comforted her through it all. After a while he felt sure their relationship was getting back on track.

Until Peter spoiled things.

She hadn't bothered to hide it. This time Tatiana had even said, 'You know things can never be the same between us since Joel. I thought I made it clear we're not a couple anymore.'

That was just something Peter had told her to say, Ross felt sure. 'How can you say that? I forgave you for Joel. Please don't leave me, those other men don't love you like I love you.'

'Sorry, I'm dating Peter.'

Peter stopped answering Tatiana's calls from that day onwards.

It wasn't long before Edwin came along. Tatiana did a good job of keeping her relationship with Edwin secret. She told Ross that she had started a college course and would be out most evenings. Ross only found out about Edwin after she'd been seeing him for a few months.

'Why didn't you tell me about him? I thought me and you were still together,' complained Ross.

'How could you think that?' said Tatiana, the disbelief clear in her eyes.

'You never gave me a reason to believe otherwise, I just thought you needed time after Peter. How could you start seeing someone else? Did you meet him at this course you're doing?'

'I wasn't doing a course. I just told you that because you always make things awkward when I bring men here. I'm sure you scare them off.'

'Why are we still living together if we're not a couple? Explain that?'

'Because we signed the tenancy when we were a couple. Thankfully there's not long to go before it ends.'

Ironically, she told Ross that Edwin had helped her get over the cruel way Peter had just "ghosted" her. She meant that in the sense of him disappearing, but had no idea how close to the truth her statement was. It made Ross think of Peter and wonder whether he was in fact a ghost now. But he didn't believe in that kind of thing.

◈

The night was turning into day and Ross had not yet dug a deep enough hole to get rid of the evidence.

After he found out about Edwin, Tatiana had brought him back home one day and introduced him to Ross. 'This is Edwin,' she'd said plainly. 'We're going out tonight, I'm just going to get changed. Can you make him a cup of coffee please? Thanks.'

Ross had been tempted to poison the coffee there and then.

Instead, he had spoken to Tatiana when she returned home from her date that night.

She seemed surprised to see him and looked at her watch. 'It's late Ross. I thought you'd be in bed.'

'About that,' said Ross, 'don't you think it's about time we started sharing a bed again?'

Tatiana blinked exaggeratedly and spluttered, 'You're kidding, right?'

'No. Look, I know things haven't been the same since Peter, well even since Joel.'

'Ross, you need to move on. You need to find someone else. The tenancy is coming to an end soon, after that we should go our separate ways. You seem to be holding on to the past.'

Ross stood up. 'Tatiana, you may not be seeing it now, but we were meant to be together. Remember how good things were before Joel came along.'

'Joel didn't come along, I started dating him because things were not great between us.'

'But he left you.'

'I'm not surprised after you made him feel awkward.'

'Peter left you too. Don't you see there's a pattern here? This new bloke, Edwin, he'll leave you too.'

'You're stuck in the past.'

'I'm still here after all those men are gone. That should tell you something.'

'Ross—'

'I love you, Tatiana.'

'I cheated on you and since then I've been dating other men, how can you say you love me?'

'I do. You've made mistakes, but I'm still here. I forgive you.'

'What?'

'You might have thought I'd be angry with you after Joel, that's why you've been dating others, isn't it? But I'm not angry. Let's just get back to where we were before, let's forget about those men as if they never existed.'

Tatiana held her head. 'I've introduced you to Edwin, for God's sake, you know I'm with him now.'

'He'll break your heart just like they did.'

'No, he won't. He's a good man.'

In the past couple of days, Tatiana had started getting closer to Ross again. She couldn't understand why Edwin had not returned her calls and was blanking her. She told Ross that she was starting to feel as though

69

there was something wrong with her because no one stayed. He'd reminded her that he had stayed. He was sure things were getting back on track now. He was trying to convince her to leave the country with him, telling her that new surroundings would help them forget the past and start again. She hadn't agreed yet, but hadn't said no. Ross knew he would have to go on the run because it wouldn't be too long before the police came sniffing around.

Ross looked at the hole in the ground. It wasn't deep enough, but it would have to do. He opened the car boot and took Edwin's body out. He managed to cover the body and seal the hole before the sun rose and felt pleased with himself.

When he got back to the car and sat in the passenger seat, he heard a notification on his mobile phone; it was a message from Tatiana.

Ross, please come home. Where are you? Sorry I took you for granted.

He smiled as he started the car and made his way back, thinking only of Tatiana and the future they would have. No one could tear them apart.

Bonus Stories

The following stories were originally featured in the Mind's Eye Series. Pictures were provided by photographers Martin David Porter, Helle Gade, and Kim Stapf. The photographs inspired the stories. Most of the books in the Mind's Eye Series are available in eBook and paperback versions, and can be found at some online retailers or ordered from your local bookstore. They are "Perspectives", "Reflections", "Triptychs", "Tales From The Cacao Tree", and "People Are Strange". The books feature stories and poems by various authors along with stunning photographs.

Love and War

'I left him here.'

'You bastard! You're supposed to be his best friend. Why the hell did you go along with it?'

'Sharon—'

'Anything could've happened to him.' She wiped the tears streaming from her eyes.

Dan hated to see her so shaken, wanted to comfort her. He put an arm around her, but she pushed him away. The rejection stabbed at his heart.

'You'd better find him.' She looked directly at him with a venom-filled stare. 'If anything's happened to him, I'll fuckin' kill you.'

'Okay, look, relax, Shaz; it was a stag night joke that went a bit wrong.'

'A bit wrong?' Her blue eyes were wide. 'My fiancé could have been eaten by wild animals or something!'

'Oh come on, Shazza, you're—'

'What? Overreacting? Getting neurotic? Bloody men! Idiots, the lot of you!' She glowered at him.

'So you're including Jeff in that?'

She pulled herself up to her full height and leaned towards him, eyes narrowed, black globules of mascara glistening in the corners. 'Don't bring him into this. He's the best thing that's ever happened to me.'

He thought she looked so beautiful with those reddened cheeks complementing her hair. 'You're too good for him, Shaz; maybe this is a blessing in disguise.'

Her mouth fell open and she took a step back. 'What?'

'If you must know, he's seeing someone else.' Dan looked at the ground. Memories of the last time he was here—with Jeff—flashed before him, and he had to close his eyes momentarily. He took a deep breath and let out a sigh.

'You're lying!' She pushed a ringlet of red hair away from her eye.

'Why would I lie?' he said, unable to meet her eyes. He held his hands palms upwards. 'What have I got to gain by lying?'

'You're just trying to—' She hesitated.

'What?' He shrugged and walked away towards the car. 'Come on, let's go. It's cold and it's getting late. Likelihood is, Jeff's back at home now wondering where we are.'

'Wait!' screamed Sharon.

Dan twisted around to face her.

'Tell me you were lying.'

He rolled his eyes. 'Okay, I was lying,' he admitted.

'I knew it, you bastard.'

Dan shook his head and took her by the hand. Her skin felt so soft. He gazed into her eyes briefly and saw her pain and wished she could feel such emotion for him, not Jeff. *Why is life so unfair?* They walked across the field back to the car.

❧❧

They sat in silence as Dan drove them home, classic rock tunes from the CD filling the void. About ten minutes into the journey, Sharon said, quite unexpectedly, 'You *were* lying, weren't you?'

'Look, it doesn't matter really, does it?' said Dan, quickly.

'What do you mean?'

'He's marrying you, isn't he?'

'You said he's seeing someone else.'

'Yeah, but he must love you if he's marrying you.'

She glared at him.

He could feel her stare burning into him, but kept his eyes fixed on the road ahead. He noticed the scent of her perfume, so sweet, and imagined her leaning in towards him, kissing him, declaring her love for him. Why did she have to fall in love with Jeff? What did Jeff have that he didn't?

After a few minutes silence, Dan glanced to his left and noticed Sharon looking out of the passenger window, watching the endless fields and desolate land drift past. He loved the way her curly hair fell down her back.

'Why the hell did you decide to bring him here?' she asked suddenly.

Dan tapped his fingers on the steering wheel, keeping the beat to the song on the CD player. 'No one likes him,' he confessed. 'He's a scumbag. He cheated on his last two girlfriends, abandoned his kids—'

'Kids? What kids?'

'Blimey! You didn't know he had kids?' He turned towards her and saw that her eyes were wide in shock, so much so that he could see the whites around the irises. He took a moment to admire how her eyes were so blue, like the sky, but almost translucent. He could get lost in those eyes. He pulled his gaze from her and looked back out of the windscreen.

'He's got three kids from his first marriage,' he continued. 'They live in Canada now with their mum. He never sees them.'

'You're lying.'

'Stop fuckin' accusing me of lying. Bloody hell, Shazza.' He gripped the steering wheel tighter and felt his cheeks redden. Why did she care so much about Jeff?

'Sorry,' she said, and then turned away to face the passenger window. 'He never told me.'

When their eyes met again a couple of minutes later, he noticed her tears. He wanted to wipe the tears away. Kiss them away.

Sharon swiped a sleeve over her face. When her arm came down he saw she'd wiped the black mascara, but stripes of it remained on her face. She reminded him of a small child who'd been practicing putting on make-up for the first time. He found it quite endearing.

'What else should I know about him?' she mumbled.

'Huh?' Dan frowned as he stared ahead at the winding country road.

'You said no one likes him. Why?'

'He's just not a very nice person.'

Sharon shook her head. 'He's always been good to me.'

'He's a charmer.'

'Why am I such a fool?' she questioned. 'Do you have any tissues in this car?'

'Yeah, in the glove compartment.' Dan sighed. 'I've gotta be honest with you, Shaz, Jeff told me he wasn't gonna show up at the wedding. I punched him when he said that.' He held his left hand towards her. 'Look, I've got bruises because of it.'

'When did he say that?'

'He was the worse for wear that night; bladdered. I told the lads I'd make sure he got home safely. That's when we had the argument, after the others left. Turns out he'd only been drinking so much 'cos he didn't want to go through with the marriage. That's why I left him here.'

'Wait.' Her brow furrowed. 'If you were on a pub crawl, how could you have driven home from here to London?'

'I took the train back. I didn't drink, though. The others thought I did. I was on non-alcoholic beer all night. I'm not much of a drinker, and I wanted to make sure the others didn't do anything to Jeff. You know what lads can be like on a stag night. Truthfully, Shazza, I was only looking out for him. Especially 'cos I know no one likes him.'

'So after you had the argument, you punched him—'

'Yeah.' Dan nodded, eyes glued to the road ahead. 'He said he wasn't going to the wedding, so I punched him. He called me loads of names and wandered off. I followed him trying to get him to see sense. It was getting dark. It's quite spooky round here in the dark, y'know.' The

75

blackness that had overwhelmed him the night of the stag do replayed in his mind. He shook his head and continued, 'That's when he basically told me to get lost and said he'd find his own way home. That's when I got the idea to leave him stranded in the field as a sort of joke.'

'Jokes are supposed to be funny.'

'Sorry, Shaz, it must be hard for you to hear all this, but I kind of wanted to teach him a lesson. You're a nice girl and he screwed you over.'

Sharon sniffed and opened the glove compartment to take out a tissue. 'What am I gonna do now?' she said.

'Well... You love him.'

'After what you've told me...'

'I don't want you to think I'm trying to turn you against him. It's really none of my business. If you two wanna make a go of it, it might work out.' He clenched his jaw.

'What? When he's been lying to me, cheating on me? I don't think so!'

Dan made an effort not to smile as he said, 'So what are you gonna do?'

'I don't know.' She began to sob.

Dan wanted to stop the car and hold her in his arms, make her feel better.

'I'm supposed to be getting married in two days. What the fuck.'

'You can stay with me until you decide what to do... er... I'll sleep on the sofa, you can have my room.' He hoped she couldn't hear the excitement in his quickened speech.

Sharon wiped her eyes with the soggy tissue. 'Thank you, Dan.' She patted his left hand while he held the gear stick. 'You're a good man.'

Dan could not help the smile that crossed his lips then. Memories of the stag night played out in his mind.

'He's bladdered,' said Dan, helping Jeff out of the pub. 'Look, I'll make sure he gets home in one piece.'

Mike, Derek, and Trevor gathered around.

'How?' asked Trevor. 'You've been drinking just as much as him, mate. It would make more sense for Derek to drive him. He—'

'No. It's okay.' Dan waved an arm to silence him. 'Do you really expect Derek to be able to deal with him in this state?'

'What the fuck?' said Jeff, eyes half closed as he leaned against Dan's shoulder. 'Where are we?'

Dan pulled him upright as he almost toppled over.

Derek shrugged. 'You could put him in the back seat, he's bound to fall asleep, then we can all drive back together.'

'No, it's okay,' said Dan.

'But you haven't got any transport. How are you gonna get him home?' chipped in Mike.

'There's a B'n'B just up the road there, we drove past it. I'm gonna check us in for the night, then we can get the train back tomorrow.'

'I don't like leaving you here,' said Derek.

'We'll be okay, I know this place,' said Dan. 'Been here a few times. I also have a friend who lives nearby. Might even be able to stay with him.' He shrugged.

'But I thought you said you'd never been this far north before,' said Derek, frowning.

'Yeah, you said that,' said Trevor.

'Yeah, well, to be honest, I can't remember what I said, I feel a bit drunk. I need a shower and a bed right now. Look, you lot go back and I'll get this one home tomorrow.'

'It's dark and it's starting to get misty,' said Derek. 'At least let me drop you off at the B'n'B.'

'No, you're all right, mate.' Dan started walking away from the group, leading Jeff with him. 'I know where the B'n'B is. It's just up this way.'

The stag party had ended up in The Griffin, a pub in a far-flung corner of the country. Dan knew they were somewhere up north. They'd been on a pub crawl, intending to drive from London to Scotland, stopping at various pubs along the way. Derek was the designated driver, grumbling for most of the journey that he missed out on all the fun.

They didn't get as far as Scotland. They called it a night when they were somewhere north of Birmingham. Dan had been on non-alcoholic drinks all evening, biding his time. He'd planned this for months. This pub was the perfect location. He'd told Derek to stop there, a stone's throw from some farmland; much of the land seemed abandoned.

Dan had fallen for Sharon the first time he met her. Love at first sight. She had the most beautiful auburn hair, the bluest eyes, and the warmest smile. She was all he'd ever dreamed of, but she loved Jeff. Jeff—his best friend.

At first Dan tried to fight the feelings, but every time he saw them together it felt as if a knife was being plunged deeper and deeper into his heart.

He began to hate Jeff. He wanted Sharon. No matter what it took to get her.

Jeff was a sensible drinker, never allowing himself to get drunk. Sensible in every other aspect of his life too. When he met Sharon, a latent jealousy had awoken in Dan. Why did Jeff always make the right moves?

Dan thought back to the mistakes he'd made in his own life; losing the custody battle for his kids ten years before. They lived with their mother in Canada now. He was lucky if he saw photos of them every Christmas. He had a history of failed relationships, had cheated on his last girlfriend.

He felt sure, though, that if he got together with Sharon he would never cheat on her. He got it into his head that they were meant for each other. He had to have her. Why should Jeff always have the best of everything? Goody two-shoes Jeff.

Dan made sure to spike Jeff's drinks that night.

ဢ

As he heard the engine start, Dan craned his neck and saw Derek, Trevor, and Mike drive off into the distance.

He pulled Jeff along the street.

'Where are we going? Why didn't we go with the others?' asked Jeff as he became lucid again for a brief moment.

'Never you mind,' said Dan, grumpily. Plans formulated in his mind as to how he could get back to London. He was sure he'd seen signs to a train station not far along the road. If the worst came to the worst he could ask back at the pub once he'd dumped Jeff.

By the time Dan dragged Jeff up the street to the abandoned farmland, his arms were aching. He felt glad there had been no one around to see him on the ten-minute walk up the hill.

He could not have wished for a better setting. As Jeff slumped to the ground at his feet, Dan took a moment to look about him. Nothing but barren land, overgrown grass, an old broken gate that had probably not seen anything pass through it for at least a hundred years.

He looked down and saw his once best friend, now sworn enemy. The man who had it all, he'd never had to struggle for one day in his whole life. Jeff was always successful. If he wanted something, be it a job, a possession, a girlfriend, he always got it.

Dan took a deep breath as he watched Jeff. He was asleep, snoring. Knocked out by the various concoctions of booze plied by Dan on the pub crawl.

Dan left Jeff on the ground and walked towards the gate to take a better look at the surroundings. The mist was really beginning to settle now. As he approached the gate, a flock of birds flew off into the distance, as if disturbed by his footsteps. He noticed an old spade next to the gate. It looked quite heavy, metallic, but rusted with age.

Dan's original plan had been to leave Jeff here—in the middle of nowhere—take his wallet and watch, and hope he didn't make it back in time for the wedding; but now he began to think that wouldn't be enough. He had to get rid of him once and for all. When Jeff didn't show for the wedding, Sharon would be left in the lurch, then Dan would comfort her and he'd finally have her for himself. Yes, Jeff had to be disposed of for good.

It seemed serendipitous to have found this the barren land and now the spade... Perhaps the universe was on his side. For once.

Dan ran back to where Jeff lay slumped. He dragged him by the feet until he was as close to the gate as possible. Then, he picked up the spade, which felt heavy in his hands.

He began to dig a hole. When he had dug about three feet into the ground, he heard Jeff begin to stir.

Jeff coughed and mumbled something, then sat up looking around him.

Dan panicked. He could not let him get away... He'd come so far, was almost there. Without thinking, he ran over to where Jeff lay still half dazed from the alcohol. 'Sorry, mate,' he muttered under his breath and then drove the hard metal edge of the spade down onto Jeff's head. Once, twice, three times. He kept pummelling, kept going, ignoring the blood, ignoring the screams... Eventually, there was no more sound, no more fight left in Jeff. Dan stopped hitting and fell to his knees. 'Sorry, mate,' he repeated over and over, breaking down in tears.

A few minutes later, he stood up and walked back to the hole he'd been digging and continued, thinking only of Sharon and the life they would have together.

No longer showing signs of remorse, he dragged his old friend's body into the freshly dug hole and covered it. By now dawn was breaking. His hands were sore, his back ached, and his head throbbed.

He walked back towards the road, trying to remember where he'd seen the sign for the train station, his head full of dreams.

Blowin' In The Wind

'Sometimes we don't end up where we were meant to be. Something stops us,' said Mr Blake. 'An obstacle, perhaps. We can remain stuck. Stuck in a place we were never meant to be. There are things in life that we want to have, but if we do, it stops the natural progression of things. They say if you love something, you have to set it free.'

Janna sat staring out of the window. She had volunteered at the old people's home on finding herself out of work. It was something to do to occupy her time. The alternative was spending endless hours alone in her studio flat with anxiety as her only friend. Money worries meant she'd drifted away from the people she used to socialise with, unable to afford the nights out. It was a struggle paying the rent on the tiny flat. Not that many invites came her way these days; funny how people don't want to know you when you're down on your luck.

Mr Blake was chatting away as usual. Janna thought he fancied himself as a bit of a guru; always spouting advice about what she should do with her life.

Today, a little girl had been playing outside the window, and Janna had mentioned it to Mr Blake. 'Oh, look, she's wishing on a dandelion... or maybe it's a thistle. Can't see it clearly.' Janna watched as the feathery white downy spores flew into the wind. Some landed on the tall grass below. 'At least she's still young enough to believe in dreams, and wishes coming true.' Janna frowned, and stopped herself, realising she was becoming a bit melodramatic, a habit she'd been slowly developing since finding herself jobless again at the age of twenty-nine.

That was when Mr Blake had started imparting his wisdom, 'Sometimes we don't end up where we're meant to be...' *Huh! That's the understatement of the century,* she thought, while smiling a fake smile at the old man. When he started going on about loving something and setting it free, she took that as her cue to leave; didn't want to end up having to listen to more clichéd sayings all joined together in an attempt to inspire and illuminate. 'God, I'm getting cynical in my old age,' she muttered to herself, while waving good-bye to old Mr Blake.

☙❧

Back at home that evening, Mr Blake's words resounded in Janna's head as she stirred her pasta. Thinking about it, she felt terrible for leaving him at that point, realising he'd sounded a bit down, as if he was trying to tell her about his own failures. She hated the way she'd become so sensitive being out of work, thinking everyone was judging her. It made her react without thinking things through properly. Perhaps Mr Blake wasn't talking about her and her job situation when he said we don't end up where we're meant to be. After all, he was in an old people's home... it was possible he was referring to his own situation. She also began to wonder what he'd meant by "They say if you love something, you have to set it free." Maybe there was a failed love affair in his past and he'd had to set someone free whom he'd really loved.

It occurred to her that she never really listened to people anymore, so caught up in her own anxieties about when she would find another job. She thought of Mr Blake all alone in that room day after day, night after night.

Regina, the manager at the old people's home, told her he rarely had visitors. *How sad*, she thought, regretting treating him and his words as so unimportant.

≫◦≪

The next day, Janna went to visit him again, even though she wasn't due back at the old people's home until the following afternoon.

'Mr Blake,' she said, settling herself beside his bed. 'Yesterday, you said something about setting things free if you love them. What did you mean by that?'

There was silence for a moment as the old man stared blankly ahead. Janna worried in case he'd gone into a catatonic state or something similar. She prodded, 'Were you talking about something that happened in your own life?'

His eyes widened. 'Who are you?' he questioned, twisting his head quickly in her direction.

She opened her mouth to speak.

'Are you a journalist, or something?'

'No... No, I—'

'I'm an old man, I can hardly remember what I do from one minute to the next, you can't expect me to remember what I said yesterday, young lady,' he said gruffly. 'Anyway, you're not supposed to be here until tomorrow. I like my routine. I always have. Tuesdays are when I usually read a book in the afternoon.'

Janna felt suddenly rejected as Mr Blake reached over to pick up a heavy tome from the bedside table.

'Thank you for visiting, but I wasn't expecting you and I can't deal

81

with sudden changes in my routine, not at my age. Sorry, dear.' With that, he began to read his book.

Janna shifted uncomfortably in the chair and then slowly stood up.

She decided to pop in to see Alice Pelton, a woman in her late eighties who always had a smile for her. Janna needed her spirits lifted. After all the times she'd visited him these past few weeks, it came as a shock to be so readily dismissed by Mr Blake. It made her feel reluctant to visit him again. This voluntary job was supposed to help build her confidence while searching for work, not bring her down.

ço~ç

'Hello, love,' said Alice as Janna approached her in the open-plan communal area at the home. The old woman's smile was bright and encouraged Janna to shake off the fear that she would be asked to leave again.

'Hi, Mrs Pelton.'

'Please, call me Alice. I'm sure I've told you to call me Alice.'

'Yes, sorry. How are you today, Alice?' asked Janna, feeling more comfortable now, sitting in the chair next to the old woman.

'Oh, mustn't grumble. I've been having the most painful neck aches recently and my hands are a bit numb.' She opened and closed her hands as if to prove a point, screwing up her face.

'Sorry to hear that,' said Janna.

'It's the old age, to be expected. Enough about me, how are you, dear? Found a job yet?'

Janna sighed. 'No. Still looking. It's tough out there. I spend hours filling in application forms, and some companies don't even bother acknowledging my letters or replying at all.'

'You keep trying, dear, and don't be discouraged by rejection. There's the right job for you out there and if it's the job meant for you, you'll get it. Just like in nature, there's a way of things, a course to follow. You'll get where you need to be, don't you worry.'

'Hmm... That's not what Mr Blake said yesterday. He said sometimes we get stuck where we're not meant to be.' Janna frowned.

Alice was silent for a while.

Janna looked at her after a couple of minutes, wondering if she might have fallen asleep. Looking at the old woman, she saw a tear in the corner of her eye.

Apparently noticing Janna turning towards her, the old woman dabbed the tear dry with a tissue.

'Are... Are you okay?' asked Janna, raising her eyebrows.

'No one has told you about Todd Blake, have they?'

'Told me about him? What should I know?'

The old woman took a deep breath and continued: 'He spent some time in prison.'

Janna's mouth fell open.

'I don't know the full story,' said Alice, 'only what I read in the newspaper, and my memory isn't very good these days.'

'What did he do?' asked Janna, intrigued.

The old woman pursed her lips. Sighing, she said, 'He became obsessed with a little girl; she was about five or six years old. He'd watch her on her way to and from school with her mum and siblings. Then one day, he lured her into his house. She wasn't found until ten years later.'

Janna put a hand over her mouth. Up until this moment, she'd thought of Mr Blake as a defenceless old man, had felt sorry for treating him badly; all of those illusions were being stripped away. 'Wow,' she said. 'I would never have imagined... old Mr Blake. I thought he was...' Her mind drifted, filled with thoughts of the times she had spent with him. It occurred to her that when she met old people all she saw was someone who needed help with this and that, someone vulnerable. She hardly ever thought of their past, their history. Of course there were criminals who are now old people. As her naivety was brought to light, her cheeks reddened.

'Well, I suppose he appears pretty normal,' said Alice. 'We can never really know what skeletons lurk in people's closets just by looking at them, though.'

'What happened to the little girl?'

'She survived. They found no signs that he'd done anything to her. He said he thought she was beautiful. He fancied himself as an artist back then, I think. They found dozens of paintings and sketches of the girl in his house.'

'How come no one knew she was there?'

'He kept her hidden in his basement.'

'Oh my God. How awful.'

'His friends and family disowned him. He was locked away for years. No one really knows what went on in that house.' The old woman shook her head and her eyes had a distant look, as if she was lost in thought.

'If you love something you have to set it free...' said Janna, remembering the words Mr Blake had spoken the day before.

'Sorry, dear?' Alice's brow creased in confusion.

'That's what he said to me yesterday. He must have been talking about the girl.'

'Emileen. That's her name,' said Alice. 'I always remember the headlines; it said when he was caught he told the press he loved the girl, so he wanted to keep her.'

'That's so creepy.' Janna wrinkled her nose.

'She visits him.'

'What?' blurted Janna. 'Are you serious?'

'Yes. Of course, no one knows it's her, but I recognise her. Years have passed, but her face hasn't changed much.'

'How often does she visit?' Janna looked around the room.

'Every couple of months. She calls him Uncle Todd.' The old woman shrugged. 'He's forty years her senior, but I read that when he got out of prison they lived together for a while.'

'What, you mean they had a relationship?'

'Yes, it seems that way.'

'How strange.'

'He never talks about her.' Alice raised her eyes skyward, then put a hand to her mouth and peered over Janna's shoulder. 'Speak of the devil,' she said, under her breath.

'Huh?' Janna twisted around to see a woman who appeared to be in her forties, standing at the reception desk. The woman was smiling at the receptionist and they seemed to be having a conversation.

A few moments later, the woman walked away towards the corridor leading to Mr Blake's room.

'Was that her?' asked Janna, eyes wide, turning back to face Alice Pelton.

The old woman nodded and raised her eyebrows. 'I asked her once why she visits.'

'Really? What did she say?'

'Her answer was, "Sometimes life doesn't work out how you planned it, but that doesn't mean it's not a good life".'

'What does that mean?' Janna screwed up her face.

'She told me she's glad she met Todd. He took her down a different path, one she would never have travelled if he hadn't snatched her away, and now it's part of her life story.'

Janna's brow furrowed as she pondered how someone who'd been kidnapped and kept a prisoner could have that attitude. She thought about the well-dressed woman who'd been standing at the reception desk. If she'd seen her in the street she would never have guessed her background. Far from looking dishevelled and miserable at having been abused, the woman looked so carefree, as if she'd had a blessed life. Alice's words floated back into her mind: *We can never really know what skeletons lurk in people's closets just by looking at them.*

Janna thought of old Mr Blake taking a small child from her family, stealing her away. She thought of their recent conversations and how she'd actually thought he sounded quite wise on occasion with his endless inspirational rants. It made her skin crawl. 'Wasn't she scared?' she said.

'I asked her that,' said Alice. 'She said she was too young to know any different. He sometimes spoke to her, in the months before he lured her away. I suppose he'd gained her trust. She thought he was a nice old man, said he was always kind to her and he was the only person she knew for ten years. Everyone wanted her to hate him, but she didn't. She said she could never hate him.'

'But isn't that just weird?'

'Maybe to you and me, darling, but if it's the only life you know, you make the most of it. I think those years created a bond between them somehow. When Todd was released from prison she went to stay with him. And now... well, she visits him. She won't hear a word said against him.' The old woman shook her head from side to side.

'So she loves him?' ventured Janna.

'It appears that way.'

'But how can she?'

'The answer is blowin' in the wind.' The old woman sniggered. 'Love has no rhyme or reason, dear. Some call it madness.'

Oblivion

Misty gazed through the telescope into the dark sky. It had become a ritual now. Every night for hours on end, she would sit here in the study where Robin used to sit. He loved this room. The walls were plastered with maps of faraway galaxies. He'd known all their names. He would talk to Misty for hours about distant stars and moons. Her mind had drifted at those times. She liked looking through his telescope and seeing the different planets, but that was the extent of her knowledge. Robin had been different. He'd been obsessed.

The room had almost become a shrine, preserved exactly as he'd left it. Misty often wondered at the expensive equipment that went with the powerful telescope; there were various different lenses and a whole host of attachments, but she hadn't a clue how to use them. He'd shown her so many different planets, and how to observe the sun safely through a special lens. She'd found it fascinating, but sometimes thought Robin's interest could be considered a bit extreme.

Twisting the body of the telescope, she peered through the lens and questioned herself for the hundredth time: *Why am I doing this?* She felt foolish knowing her dream was that one day, she might see Robin through this telescope. Find him again. Maybe he would find a way to send a sign.

A part of her had disappeared with him, she felt sure of it. A part of her sanity. Otherwise, why would she even be entertaining such thoughts? But no logical explanation could be found, so the conundrum kept bouncing off the sides of her brain, like balls in a pinball machine, never finding their way out, never quite accessing an answer.

The most overwhelming thing had been the darkness. The black, impenetrable denseness. Whenever Misty thought back to what had happened, her mind could not pierce through the blackness. Her introspection did nothing more than shine a light on the dark; a light that merely hovered above it, not quite breaking through, only revealing mist and more layers of oblivion. Nothingness. Somehow, however, she sensed there was something underneath. Memories floated just above, trying to penetrate. Failing. Unmistakably red—there had been a definite tinge of red—but like the rest of the detail this remained locked away, out of reach, only a hint of it nagging at her brain.

They'd been walking together and wandered off the path. Robin said it would be easy enough to find their way back to the main road, but he'd always been an adventurer. He'd wanted to find out what lay beyond the vastness of the mountain range, wanted to discover something not yet seen by human eyes. His mission in life had always been to seek out the new and be the first to do something, stand out from the crowd. Always searching. She'd loved that about him, but now she would probably spend the rest of her days searching for him.

ೊಀ

'Maybe we should get back to the main road,' said Misty, shivering. The temperature had suddenly dropped as they wandered further from the trail.

'I just want to have a look up here,' said Robin, map in hand, compass at the ready.

'It'll start getting dark soon, Rob,' Misty warned.

'We have a torch,' he said, pulling her by the hand. 'Stop being such a scaredy-cat.'

'I'm not, but we don't know this place.'

ೊಀ

They'd travelled together for a while now, both taken extended leave from their jobs. Neither of them found the nine-to-five lifestyle much fun. Both loved adventure. They'd been to many long-haul destinations every year for two weeks at a time on their annual holidays, but Robin always said he wanted to take more time to travel. He said life was too short to stay in one place. 'There's a whole universe out there, waiting to be explored,' had been his mantra. One of his dreams had been to discover a new planet.

Robin always seemed to be itching to get away from wherever he found himself. He never settled in one job too long. Misty's mother often said he had 'ants in his pants'.

Surprisingly, for the five years prior to their last holiday, he'd worked at the same company, and Misty began to think he might be starting to settle down as he got older. Then he got the idea about taking a long holiday.

ೊಀ

Robin continued walking further and further off the track.

The mist began to gather around them as the sun began its descent.

'I'm worried we won't be able to find our way back, Rob!'

'Stop worrying, we have a compass.'

There was something unnerving about the vastness of space around them with no other soul in sight, as if they were the only two people left on Earth.

The mountain on either side of them began to appear imposing to Misty. Holding tighter to Robin's hand, she said, 'There's nothing here, Rob, let's get back.'

He stopped walking and looked around. 'Hmm... maybe you're right. There's not much to see.'

The daylight began to fade quite suddenly then, and Misty turned to Robin, wide-eyed.

'Wow! It's getting dark quickly, isn't it?' he said.

'Ye-yes,' she agreed, peering ahead warily.

They heard a low humming noise.

'What's that?' asked Misty.

'Um. I'm not sure. Maybe there are animals around here. Come on, let's get back.'

As they walked along at a quickened pace back towards the road, their breathing became heavier. The only sound other than their breathing and the trudging of their boots, was the deep humming, and it seemed to be getting louder.

Then darkness fell; not in the way that night usually comes about, but more like a blanket of darkness falling on top of them, shutting out all light except from a red beam hovering above the dark.

'Rob! Rob!' screamed Misty.

'Don't panic,' he said.

Misty saw a glow emerging from where Robin stood and at first it frightened her, but then realising it was the torch, she let out a sigh. Her relief was short-lived: strangely, the torch did nothing to penetrate the dark, just threw a beam of light into it, revealing layers of mist.

Robin's hand slipped from hers.

'Rob!'

The loud humming had increased and became almost deafening, sounding as though it was directly above them.

Glancing up, Misty saw a light so bright she had to close her eyes. On opening them, she saw the luminescence waning, and the red tinge moving away into the darkness above. Immediately after that, the sky cleared and daylight resumed, just as it had been before the blanket of night had fallen, as if someone had flicked a switch. Misty was standing alone. Robin had vanished.

Misty ran back to the main road, and seeing a taxi jumped in front of it, not even thinking of the risk of being run over. She tried to explain to the driver, but he didn't speak much English, didn't understand, so she asked him to drive her to the hotel.

Once at the hotel, she alerted the authorities.

A search party was sent out.

They never found Robin.

It remained a mystery.

Misty pulled her eye from the telescope and rubbed it, stifling a yawn. Looking at the clock she saw it was already 2 a.m. Time for bed. She could try again tomorrow. Maybe one day she would find him.

Repercussions

Eight-year-old Reggie wished on the dandelion and watched the fluffy seeds fly off into the wind, tears streaming down his cheeks.

'What shall we do with that one?' asked Damson as he watched the boy trundle off back into the house.

'Well, his wish was a bit extreme. T'was fuelled by anger. We cannot grant it. It would go against all fairy wisdom,' replied Apple-Blossom.

Damson frowned. 'But... he seemed very upset. Isn't there anything we can do?'

Apple-Blossom twisted a lock of golden hair around her finger and surveyed Damson with a glimmer of gentle thoughtfulness in her yellow-green eyes. 'Sometimes it's hard being a dandelion fairy, but that's what your training is for. You have to be able to recognise the soul's wishes. The pure ones.' She fluttered her golden wings getting ready to leave. 'If we grant this boy's wish, it would cause all sorts of repercussions. One negative action leads to another.'

'Like karma, you mean?'

The little fairy thought for a while, eyes narrowed. 'Yes,' she said eventually. 'Just like karma, I s'pose.' With that, Apple-Blossom gave a final flutter of her wings and hovered above the branch of the tree. 'C'mon, I can hear some more dandelion seeds in the air. Over there.' She reached out an arm and pointed with a sparkly green fingernail. 'Can you see the girl with the hat? Let's go and find out what she's wishing for.'

❧❧

Reggie walked back into the kitchen.

'Crybaby,' said Julian, his older brother.

'Shut up!' said Reggie, thinking of the wish he'd made and wondering how long it would take to come true.

'You shut up,' replied Julian, sticking out his tongue.

'Stop fighting, you two,' said their mother while stirring the soup she was preparing for dinner.

Reggie stormed out of the kitchen and ran upstairs to the bedroom he shared with Julian, slamming the door behind him.

Sitting down on the edge of his bed, he swiped the relentless tears with the sleeve of his shirt. *I should have wished he would die.*

As the two fairies flew away towards the girl, Damson said, 'Couldn't we have helped the boy in any way?'

'No,' replied Apple-Blossom. 'Once a wish is made, it's made. We either grant it or dismiss it. We can't start making our own decisions about what someone should have wished for. That's not our job, and it would be against the fairy code of honour.'

Damson nodded, but thoughts of the young boy's tears remained in his mind's eye.

Soon, they arrived at where the girl stood, and listened to her wish. Although she didn't speak it, the fairies were able to feel the vibration of her desires floating on the wind with the dandelion seeds.

'I wish Roy would fall in love with me,' came the wish on the breeze.

'Hmm...' said Apple-Blossom. 'We call this the anti-love wish'

'Anti-love?' queried Damson. 'How? It sounds like she's in love with Roy.'

'Perchance she is, but we don't grant this category of wishes.'

'Why not?'

'Because they're against the laws of nature.'

Damson let out a disappointed grunt. So far today, there had been wishes that were considered obstructive to personal growth, a few contrary to the fairy code, and now this one: against the laws of nature.

'I don't understand why this is against the laws of nature,' he complained. 'She loves this man. Maybe he needs a bit of a nudge in the right direction?' Damson fluttered his shiny purple wings and moved closer to Apple-Blossom as he said, 'I signed up to be a dandelion fairy because I want to help people.'

'Believe me, Damson, you have much to learn about helping.' Apple-Blossom touched him softly on the arm 'Sometimes the best way to help is by doing nothing at all.' Then she frowned at him, 'Be patient, boy. Many a fairy has floundered by being too keen to do good.'

Damson sighed. 'Please explain, Apple-Blossom, so I can understand: how can love be against the laws of nature?'

'Love has a time and a reason. We cannot interfere.'

'Are there any wishes that we *can* grant?' he asked, rolling his amethyst-coloured eyes and placing a hand under his chin.

'Have I taught you nothing today?' grumbled Apple-Blossom, raising her eyebrows. 'The *only* wishes we can grant are the soul's wishes.

You'll know one when you hear it. Trust me.'

'I can't stop thinking about that little boy... crying,' said Damson, thinking aloud.

'Hmm... you'll never make a dandelion fairy if you get emotionally involved,' chided Apple-Blossom.

'I just think—'

'Your opinion is neither here nor there, young fairy. You must follow the code and the laws of nature. C'mon, there's another wish not too far away. Follow me.'

⊱⊰

Later that evening, Damson watched as Apple-Blossom took a nap. They were under the oak tree, not too far from the house where little Reggie lived.

Damson felt disappointed that on his first day as a trainee dandelion fairy not one wish had been granted. This wasn't what he'd signed up for. He wanted to make dreams come true, to make people happy.

Surely it would make more sense to grant wishes when people really wanted them, spread more joy, make people smile when they were at their lowest ebb? He could still see Reggie's little face, tears streaming down. It had upset him.

Maybe I could grant this one wish, he thought mischievously. *After all, what his brother did was horrible. Justice should be seen to be done.*

Apple-Blossom was fast asleep.

Damson took the opportunity to speed away, estimating it would only take him ten minutes to fly there, grant the wish, and fly back. She'd never know.

He recalled Reggie's wish: *'I wish Julian would fall down the stairs and break his legs.'*

Hmm... Yes, it is a bit harsh, thought Damson, but because of his fairy wisdom he was aware of the reason Reggie had made the wish: Julian had pushed him down the stairs and laughed when Reggie cried. *It won't do any harm*, the fairy thought to himself. *I'll grant the bit about him falling down the stairs, but not breaking his legs... maybe just a few cuts and bruises.* He sniggered.

Damson fluttered outside the boys' bedroom window and pulled the magic wand from his belt. He cast a spell to make Julian thirsty so he'd have to go downstairs for a drink.

The little fairy then waved his wand to move a few toys and

strategically place them at the top of the stairs.

Feeling proud of himself, he fluttered away, wishing he could stay to see Reggie's little face light up when his cruel brother tripped and fell; but he had to get back to Apple-Blossom before she awoke.

❧

'Go and get me a glass of water,' said twelve-year-old Julian.

'You go,' said Reggie, who was about to climb into his bed.

'I'm already in bed,' moaned Julian. 'And, besides, I'm older; you have to listen to me.'

'I'm not going.'

'Scaredy-cat.'

'I'm not scared!'

'So prove it. I dare you to go downstairs and get me a glass of water without switching the hall light on.'

'Huh! You just want me to get your water.'

'Told you you're scared,' said Julian, as he pushed back his duvet to climb out of bed.

'I'm not scared,' protested Reggie. 'Okay, I'll go and get your stupid water.'

Reggie ran out of the room and toppled down the stairs, tripping over a toy robot and twisting his ankle.

Julian stood laughing at the top of the staircase.

On the Rocks

The first time Ellie saw Sean he was playing a guitar. Music was her first love, and she'd always loved any music featuring a guitar. Something about the sound it made set off a vibration deep within her soul.

Ellie and her friend Esme had gone to see Sean's band play at a local "battle of the bands" contest. Esme's boyfriend knew Sean and wanted to support him.

A kind of magic pervaded the air when Ellie first saw Sean. She wasn't sure if it was the hypnotic effect of the music and the high energy of the crowd around her, but an electric aura permeated the evening.

At the age of twenty-one, it felt like love at first sight to Ellie; almost as if a thousand voices in the air around her whispered that he was "the one". Inexplicably, she recognised him straight away, as if she'd known him in a previous life. As they'd walked over to the main stage, her friend Esme had said, 'Sean's the one on the right, playing the guitar.' Ellie answered, 'I know,' and surprised herself with the reply, not sure why she'd said that... Such was the mystical quality of their first meeting.

Watching him play, their future seemed somehow fated; they were destined to be together—she felt sure of that.

They didn't get to chat that evening, with all the commotion over the contest in the busy pub; but the following week, Esme invited her to a dinner party. As luck would have it, Sean was there, and they chatted all evening. Ellie relaxed in his company. They had lots in common, the love of the guitar being top of the list. She confessed she'd always wanted to learn how to play the instrument.

'I'll teach you,' said Sean, smiling brightly.

'Would you?' Ellie thought his bright blue eyes looked so beautiful, she could hardly keep from staring. Wiping the corner of her mouth with a napkin, she continued, 'That would be so great. I have to warn you, though, I've only ever tried to play once before and I was a bit rubbish. But I managed to teach myself to play the first few chords of *Fast Car*... you know, the Tracy Chapman song. I felt quite proud of myself for that.' She giggled.

He remained silent, just stared.

Ellie wondered whether she'd babbled on for too long. Did he think she was a dizzy blonde?

After a brief moment, he said, 'I'd love to teach you. Sounds like you have a good ear.'

Over the next few weeks Ellie had a few guitar lessons, and got on very well with Sean. The memories she had of those days were always of them laughing and talking about everything under the sun. They agreed on most things, and she felt blessed to have found a kindred spirit.

For the next few months they were inseparable.

They married within a year of first meeting.

Looking back, those times spent with Sean in his one-bedroom flat with the stained carpets, damp wallpaper, and fish 'n' chips suppers, were the best times they'd ever shared together. All they had to live on was love. It had been enough... Once.

Over the next couple of years, Sean's band became ever more popular in the local area. Ellie attended the gigs and felt so proud to be the girl by his side; never even remotely threatened by any of the women who scrabbled for Sean's autograph. It was all a lot of fun, but he hadn't hit the big time. Yet.

When Leila, their daughter, was born, Ellie took a back seat and stayed at home, looking after the baby, no longer attending all the gigs.

Sometimes she wondered if her absence at the same time as his band being invited to play larger venues may have driven a wedge between them. But they'd planned for a baby and he'd said he was looking forward to becoming a dad. Ellie could count on her fingers the times he'd been there for their daughter in the past six years.

Almost ten years to the day she'd first met Sean, Ellie stood sneering at a recent photograph of him playing his guitar.

A tear came to her eye as she looked around the expensive home they'd moved into five years earlier when Sean's band was flying high at number one in the charts in the UK and in many other countries.

They'd enjoyed years of luxury living off the royalties, but for the past couple of years their good luck felt more like a burden than a blessing. The more successful the band became, the less time Sean had for

Ellie and Leila. It was always 'the band this' and 'the band that'. He may as well have been married to the band as far as she was concerned. A polygamous marriage wasn't something she'd signed up for.

Nowadays, they only communicated via e-mail, and squeezed in the odd Skype conversation on his days off.

Endless photographs in the music press showed Sean smiling, surrounded by beautiful-looking women. In the video for their last single, he'd kissed a well-known, stunningly gorgeous actress. Ellie found it upsetting to watch. It tore at her heart. The distance between them was widening; they didn't have much in common anymore.

Gone were the days when she'd contact him by phone or e-mail and get an instant reply. Now she'd often wait twenty-four hours for a response, while he partied in some distant land, places she'd never heard of. It irked her that she was never invited to join him. 'It's my job,' he'd say. 'I don't ask to come to the office with you, do I?'

He apologised often. Most of their conversations these days revolved around how he was sorry he couldn't make it to this or that, and how he'd missed birthdays, Christmas, or even Valentine's Day. He would always end their chats with, 'You know I love you.' The truth was, she didn't know that. Not anymore. Sean seemed to have disappeared into a parallel universe, checking in to the real world once in a while, but never for very long.

Then the rumours started in the newspapers. He'd been spotted with the actress from his music video, having fun in a restaurant; "canoodling" is what the news story had said. The pictures made Ellie's stomach turn. The actress was married too, but her marriage had been on the rocks for some time.

The final straw came when Ellie saw his photo in the paper kissing the actress's cheek. He looked a bit dazed, as if drunk; hardly recognisable as the Sean she'd fallen in love with. He'd morphed into a wayward rock star, just like those he'd admired over the years. *Is that how they all end up?* she mused bitterly.

Ellie had tried to get through to him on Skype and e-mail for the past three days, with no reply. She was sick of trying.

'Come on, Leila, we're going,' she called out.

Six-year-old Leila ran towards her. Those blue eyes and golden curls were so similar to Sean's. Ellie blinked away a tear. Every time she looked at Leila she'd be doomed to remember him. Maybe one day she'd only remember the good times, without the bitter resentment biting.

Shaking her head to rid it of the cloud-like melancholia, Ellie said,

'We're going to stay with Grandma and Grandpa for a little while, then we'll look for a new home of our own.'

'Okay, Mummy.'

Leila hardly had the chance to get to know her dad over the years, so Ellie wasn't surprised she hadn't asked about him.

He probably won't even realise we're gone, thought Ellie as she took hold of the suitcase trolley handle with one hand and Leila's hand with the other, and walked out of the door.

'Goodbye, Sean,' she whispered, pulling the door closed behind her.

Secrets of the Forest

After a day of trekking through the forest, Annette decided to have a lie in.

'We're heading off now,' said Poppy, peeking through into Annette's tent.

'Go without me; I'll catch up in a bit,' she mumbled.

Poppy frowned. 'Are you sure?'

'Yes!' snapped Annette, pulling the sleeping bag closer.

'Okay, look, we'll be heading north. You've got a compass, right?'

Annette sighed. 'Yeah. I'm only gonna snooze for about five minutes, then I'll follow.'

'Okay, head north. I'm not sure if our phones'll work out here, but you can try. If we don't hear from you in about an hour, we'll head back.'

'No need. I'll catch up.' Annette wished Poppy would just go and let her have five more minutes sleep.

'Are you sure? D'you want us to wait for you?'

'No! Look, let me sleep for a bit, I'm knackered.'

Poppy rolled her eyes.

Annette wondered why she'd ever agreed to come here with Poppy and the gang. Camping was so uncomfortable.

As the chatter and the footsteps of her friends faded away into the distance, Annette was suddenly overcome by fear, all alone in the tent. *What if I can't find them, or get lost in the forest?* Stretching her arms, she struggled to lift herself up out of the sleeping bag, but weariness dragged her down. *Five more minutes,* she thought, *then I'll get up and follow them.*

Her feet ached and her legs felt stiff. They'd walked for what seemed like miles the day before. Once again, she regretted joining the girls on the camping weekend.

As much as she wanted to rest, Annette knew that the longer she dallied here, the more stressful it would be trying to find her friends. Sighing, she forced herself to sit up. Exhaustion overwhelmed her just thinking about walking through the forest again. Lying down, to make the most of the last few minutes of rest, she made the mistake of closing her eyes and drifted off to sleep unawares.

Almost an hour later, Annette awoke and sat up in a panic, praying she'd only snoozed for a few minutes. Noticing the time on her watch, her mouth fell open. 'It can't be!'

She shot out of the sleeping bag as if someone had set fire to it, almost falling over at the sudden movement. Stars before her eyes, she took deep breaths to calm herself down. *I'll find them... they're probably on their way back, anyway; Poppy said they'd come back if I didn't follow after an hour...*

Her heart beating fast, she pulled on a clean T-shirt and pair of jeans and began to pack up the tent. She forced herself to eat a few baked beans, but her stomach was turning over. The vast expanse of the forest seemed frightening now, facing it all on her own.

In every direction there were trees... nothing but trees. No pathway, no track. She didn't know which way the girls had gone. 'Oh no!' she said aloud. 'Shit, shit, shit. Okay... north... the compass.'

Finding her compass, Annette began to head north. Unable to think straight, she hoped that she'd remembered it correctly. *Poppy said "north"... she did say "north".* A deep frown settled on her brow.

Walking quickly, trying to avoid tripping on twigs and fallen branches that lay strewn all around, it felt more like she was trying to escape from somewhere rather than enjoying a weekend break in the woods. She shivered at the thought that anyone could be hiding behind one of the trees. Her mind conjured up scenes from old horror movies where people were chased through dense forests. A paranoia took over and she began to run faster as if sensing someone behind her. Every noise became the footfalls of a madman. After just ten minutes, fatigue took hold. It was an effort to even stand in one place on her painful feet, walking further was not feasible.

Finding a log, she sat down. Her head hurt, and she knew that was probably caused by the constant tension and worry.

There was nothing to indicate whether she was getting closer to her friends. She was starting to think the compass might be faulty, directing her in circles rather than straight ahead. It was hard to tell one place from another. This log looked familiar. Putting her head in her hands, she wished for the tenth time that morning that she'd never agreed to go along with Poppy, Liza, and Frieda. She longed for home comforts: a warm bed, a pillow... Things she had taken for granted now seemed like an impossible dream.

Just then, there was a noise in the trees above. Craning her neck, she saw a large bird. Was it a crow? Recalling everything she'd heard about the birds in fantasy tales, her mind was temporarily distracted from the pain she felt. Crows were meant to be magical, mystical birds. *If only it could magic me out of the forest,* she thought wearily, head bowed.

When she looked back up at the tree, the crow had gone, seemingly vanished. Annette shrugged. Somehow, it had been comforting to have another living creature around, but now it was gone. She was alone once more.

There was a rustling from behind one of the trees. Annette jumped up, on her guard, knowing there could be dangerous animals lurking in the woods.

A man wearing a long black coat walked out from behind the tree and tipped his tall black hat towards her.

Annette thought his attire was a bit strange; old-fashioned. He looked like someone from a Charles Dickens novel. He had long black hair beneath his hat. Somehow, she didn't feel frightened of him, more fascinated.

'Cantan at your service, ma'am,' he said, with a bright smile.

'Who? What?'

'You asked me to magic you out of the forest.'

She stared wide-eyed at the man. 'I-I didn't ask... I've never seen you before...'

He laughed. 'Oh, sorry! I'm forgetting myself. When you first saw me I was a crow. Your belief in the magic of the forest has helped transform me into my human form for a time so I may assist you.'

'You were the... the cr-crow?' She stumbled over her words.

'Many moons ago, I was just like you, but I was murdered in these here woods.'

Annette gasped.

'Fear not,' said Cantan, 'you are safe here.'

'B-b-but—'

Cantan shook his head slowly. 'I protect visitors to these woods. The ones who believe in the magic.'

His smile and gentle gaze brought comfort, as if he held the power to heal with just a look from his jet black eyes. Annette's fear diminished as she gazed at this strange man. She felt her whole body relax.

'My enemy is a spirit who enjoys leading visitors to the forest astray, so that they will lose their way,' continued Cantan, 'My mission is to help those who become lost. Please do not be afraid. I mean no harm.'

Annette gulped and said, 'S-s-so you can help me find my friends?' Annette wondered whether she'd become delirious due to the pain and exhaustion, or perhaps this was just a dream and she was still asleep in the tent.

Cantan nodded and tilted his hat again. 'I will now leave you, ma'am, but if you follow the crow you will find your friends. You'll forget this meeting ever happened. The secrets of the forest must remain just so. Good day.' With a final tilt of his hat, he smiled and then disappeared behind the trees.

Annette followed where he had gone, but there was no sign of him. The crow's caw could be heard above. Annette's heart skipped a beat and she looked up. Sure enough, the crow had reappeared. It flew onto a tree to her right. Shaking her head, she thought, *This is silly*; but something compelled her to follow the bird.

Strangely, all the tiredness and the pain in her feet and legs had gone. A renewed energy coursed through her.

After walking for quite a while, following where the crow led, voices could be heard in the distance. It wasn't long before she'd caught up with the others. They were sitting on a log in a clearing that appeared similar to the place she had stopped to rest. She thought back to that mysterious place. Somehow, after only a few minutes there, she'd recovered her vitality. She still couldn't understand it. It was like she'd ventured into some sort of energy field that had revived her.

'Hey, Annette,' called out Poppy. 'We thought you'd got lost!'

'You're looking very refreshed now, I wish I'd have slept in longer,' complained Liza.

'I do feel refreshed,' said Annette, 'but it's more to do with the walk, I think. It's very strange. When I woke up, my legs and feet were aching, but I was scared of being alone in the forest so I forced myself to follow you. I was so shattered, I had to sit on a log, couldn't drag myself any further. I swear that log must've had some kind of special power. I feel like I could run a marathon now!' She jumped up and down as if to prove a point.

The girls laughed.

'You'll have to show us where it is,' said Liza. 'My legs are falling off. Don't think I can walk much further, let alone run.'

'Me neither,' said Frieda.

'I'm glad you got here. Saves us having to go back,' said Poppy. 'We were just stopping to have some lunch, then we were gonna to head back to get you.'

'Lunch sounds good. I'm starving,' said Annette.

'We've got some sandwiches,' said Poppy, opening her backpack.

'So, did you have any trouble finding us?' asked Frieda.

Annette thought about it for a minute. In her mind, she had just followed the compass north. The memories she had were of wonderful, peaceful forest scenery along the journey. 'I just followed the compass. It was easy. It's such a beautiful forest.'

'I know. It's magical, isn't it?' commented Poppy.

Something flickered in Annette's mind on hearing the word "magical", like a light turning on and off, but too quickly for her to acknowledge. She smiled at the others, as distant memories danced through her subconscious, adding a twinkle to her eye. With a nod, she said, 'Yes... Magical.'

Shadows

As the clouds hovered above the mountains they cast a black shadow in stark contrast to the white snow-capped peaks that gave this mountain range its picturesque quality. Anna could hardly bear to look at the black shadow. It appeared to taunt her.

'Are you okay, darling?' asked Paul.

She turned towards him and blinked.

'You were miles away,' he commented, pecking her cheek and passing her a glass of champagne.

They were seated at a table on the balcony of their hotel room. The view was glorious. Nothing but mountains for miles around. The expanse of the mountain range seemed endless. Such beautiful scenery, but all Anna could see were the shadows caused by the hovering clouds like ghosts in her mind, spoiling the perfect picture.

'I'm fine,' she said, snapping back to the present and reaching out a hand to offer a celebratory clink of her glass against his. This was, after all, a time for celebration. Their twentieth wedding anniversary. A twentieth anniversary, she'd discovered in a Google search, happened to be the China Anniversary where it was traditional for couples to buy gifts for each other made of china or glass. Her first thought on reading that was, *China and glass are breakable.* Knowing they would be travelling here, she couldn't help feeling concerned in case it might be some kind of omen. A deep sense of foreboding had consumed her ever since.

'Here's to us!' she said, as brightly as possible.

'To us!' said Paul, with a clink of his glass against hers.

Paul had brought them back to the mountain resort where they'd spent their honeymoon.

Anna tried to keep her eyes averted from the mountains, instead fixing her gaze on Paul. Avoiding his eyes, she focussed on his hair and recalled how black it had been the last time they were here. Now it was mostly grey and white, although there were still remnants of the once lustrous dark hair in between. Once again, she was reminded of the mountains. Instead of distracting herself from her oppressive thoughts, here they were again. The varying shades and colours in his hair mirrored those of the mountains. All she could concentrate on was the blackness. She felt the need to close her eyes.

'Are you sure you're okay, sweetheart? You've hardly said a word since we arrived.'

She opened her eyes to see Paul frowning. 'It must be the jet lag,' she said, looking down at her skirt and swiping a hand across it, as if to wipe away some dust or a crumb.

'Are you hungry?' he asked. 'Let's go to that restaurant we ate at on our honeymoon, "Starlights". I looked it up on the Internet. It's still here! I wonder if it's the same family running it now. What were their names? Isla and Rolf?'

'Isla and Ralph,' said Anna, her mind flashing back to the candle-lit restaurant where they had spent the last couple of nights of their honeymoon.

'Yes, that's right, you have a great memory. Wouldn't it be nice to see them again?'

Anna once again closed her eyes briefly. 'I'm feeling a bit tired.' Faking a yawn behind a limp hand, she wondered why she'd agreed to this trip.

ঔৣ৶

When Paul first mentioned coming back, she had shuddered. Her first words had been, 'What? No, we can't go back there.' He'd frowned and awaited an explanation. She didn't have one, not one she could tell him, so she said, 'We're old now. It's cold there. Wouldn't you prefer somewhere warm... A beach? Or better still, why not stay in England? There are some lovely country cottages we could rent, Sarah was telling me about them—'

'Country cottages?' he spluttered. 'And speak for yourself, forty-five isn't old. We're not exactly pensioners. I thought you'd liked it there. I've got such great memories of our honeymoon. It's our twentieth anniversary, Anna.' He hung his head. 'Besides,' he looked up coyly, 'I've already booked it.'

Anna placed a hand on her throat and gasped.

He continued: 'Look, I know we're not as young as we used to be. We don't have to go skiing or mountain climbing like we did last time. I've booked the same hotel we stayed at, and even the same room, can you believe it?' His eyes were wide and sparkling, filled with nostalgia.

She stood up to face him. 'Can you hear yourself? You can't go back in time and make everything the same, you know.' Tears spiked in her eyes. She turned away from him, not wanting him to see her cry.

'Darling, what's wrong?'

Walking away towards the door, she felt his hand on her shoulder.

'What did you mean by that? You're making me nervous. Have I done something to upset you? We're still okay, aren't we... I mean, I know we've been married twenty years, so things can't be perfect all the time, but...'

There was a sadness in his voice. 'It's not about us,' she sighed. 'It's about the holiday. I don't want to go there.'

'I can cancel the booking.'

She could hear the dejection in his voice. Anna began to see things through his eyes. He was unaware of what had happened back then; she'd kept it to herself. Looking at it another way, maybe it would do her good to return... Maybe she could find a way to come to terms with it all. It had been a burden for the past twenty years. Perhaps seeing it again now, from a different perspective, she could forget. They were older now, after all. 'Sorry. No, let's go,' she managed to say. 'It might do us both good.' Still unable to face him, she eventually pulled away, went upstairs, and cried for a while. The more she thought about it, perhaps it would be better to finally face her demons.

୨∞ଡ଼

So here they were, both with their own disparate memories of the honeymoon: his mostly of the fun they'd had; hers tinged with black.

'I'm going to lie down for a bit,' Anna said.

'Okay.' Paul looked at his watch. 'It's early. I'll wake you up in a couple of hours and we'll go out and get something to eat.'

She nodded and walked away.

Approaching the bed, she wondered if it could be the same one they'd slept in twenty years ago. Recollections flooded forth.

Three days into their honeymoon, Paul had been consigned to bed for a day having sprained an ankle on a mountain trek they'd been on. They'd planned a day trip. She ended up going alone. 'No sense in us both missing out,' he'd said. 'Besides, we've paid for it as part of the package deal. You go along and make sure you take lots of photos. We should've brought the camcorder, really.' He rolled his eyes.

So Anna left him. She'd met up with the couple from the next room, Josie and Reed; they'd offered to keep her company when they heard Paul wasn't able to go. She couldn't even remember what they looked liked now. Faceless people from the past. What she could remember was that she found them tiresome; constantly bickering and complaining about everything. Anna deliberately drifted away from them during the course of the day, finding a man who was alone. Vincent. He looked as lost as she felt, so she was glad to keep him company. She'd been twenty-five then. He'd appeared older, around thirty. He'd explained that he'd broken up with a long-term partner and had booked the trip for a change of scenery, to take his mind off everything.

The day trip organised by the tour company was a hike across some of the mountains to get good views of the snow-capped peaks.

Anna and Vincent got on well and spent a pleasant day together.

When the day trip was over and the coach dropped them off, Anna realised Vincent was staying at the same hotel. He invited her to his room for a drink.

'I have to check on Paul.'

'You can bring your fella as well,' Vincent said.

When Anna returned to her hotel room, she found Paul fast asleep, so she decided to go and have a drink with Vincent.

Between them they drank two bottles of red wine as Vincent told Anna all about his failed relationship and cried a couple of times. She felt sorry for him and stayed longer to comfort him.

'Sometimes I get these really black moods,' he explained. 'It's weird because it can be sunny outside but I'm locked in darkness.' He pointed to his head. 'It's all in here.'

'M-maybe you should see someone... A doctor.'

He stared blankly out of the hotel window and pointed at the mountain range beyond. 'You see those clouds, how they drift by and their shadow turns the mountains black, that's what it's like,' he mumbled.

Anna frowned. 'Promise me you'll go and see a doctor when you get back home. It sounds like you could be depressed.'

He laughed. 'I'm sure I have another bottle of red somewhere.' He stood up and nearly fell over.

'Um... I think we've both had enough already.' She helped him back onto the chair beside the window.

His blue eyes seemed to be reaching out to her. He leaned in and kissed her on the mouth.

She pulled away. 'I'm sorry... I'm married.'

'Don't apologise. We all make mistakes.' He laughed at the joke.

She stood up and suddenly felt more sober. 'No... I'm sorry. I have to go.'

'They all leave in the end,' he said morosely.

Frowning, she grabbed her coat from the back of the door and left.

ς∞๑

Vincent was found hanged in his hotel room the next day. Anna had always felt guilty about perhaps unconsciously leading him on. He'd been so broken after his failed relationship. Had she offered him a lifeline only to pull it away?

'Bloke in room nineteen has killed himself,' Paul said, after asking the hotel reception why there was a police car and an ambulance outside the building.

Anna turned white.

'What's wrong, love?' Paul had stared at her with wide eyes and concern evident in his furrowed brow.

'I met him yesterday on the trip...' she said, then put a hand over her mouth. 'So sad...' A tear came to her eye.

'It is sad.' Paul nodded. 'C'mon, we're going to be late for the skiing, bus leaves in five minutes.'

They never spoke of Vincent again, but he often haunted Anna's dreams.

Escape

It started with a snarky remark made by a colleague about a news item Petros hadn't heard about: 'Where've you been? Under a rock?' Sylvester sniggered at the comment as if it was the funniest joke he'd ever heard.

Sylvester always laughed at his own jokes. Petros wasn't entirely sure why he'd taken an instant dislike to the man, but he couldn't get his head around Sylvester's constant need to talk and be heard as if his whole life revolved around being part of the team at this dead-end customer service centre.

Petros often wondered whether the reason he didn't like him was simply because Sylvester had got the job he'd applied for. They'd gone up against each other at interview for the internally advertised position which was one step up from Petros's current role. Instead of Customer Service Assistant, which was basically answering phones all day, it was Customer Service Officer, in essence the same thing, but with the dubious benefit of being able to sit in on management meetings and supervise the new support staff who were routinely taken on and fired at intervals. It paid two thousand pounds more than the Assistant role. Sylvester, with his ability to "talk for England", had snagged the job and moved from another department into Petros's department. Sylvester never knew Petros had applied for his role, mainly because Sylvester didn't take an interest in other people; he was happy as long as he could talk all day and he liked his colleagues to agree with him.

Petros mostly ignored him, but that had the effect of making him something of a curio in Sylvester's eyes, as if the man were constantly on a mission to find a topic to talk about that would glean a positive response from Petros. Whenever Petros agreed with him, it seemed to make Sylvester feel validated on some level.

On the odd occasion that Sylvester did manage to rope Petros into a conversation, Petros was inevitably left feeling harassed. Sylvester either had no clue about the subtleties of body language and couldn't pick up on obvious hints that a conversation had ended, or he was deliberately trying to annoy Petros. Either way, Petros could only sigh and wish he was miles away. He concluded that he probably wouldn't have liked Sylvester no matter what the circumstances of their meeting.

The more Petros thought about it, the more he realised he wouldn't have been happy even if he had been successful in his application for the Customer Service Officer vacancy. It would only have been one more step up a ladder in the wrong direction.

Petros ideally wanted to leave the call centre. He hated the constant ringing of the phones. Sometimes when he lay his head on his pillow to sleep at night, there would be a buzzing sound echoing the tone of the phones reverberating in his head, like a bothersome housefly that he tried to swat, always out of reach.

Sometimes, in the office, he would not even have the chance to catch his breath after a phone call before another one came through. He found it increasingly difficult to answer the phone in a professional and courteous manner, especially after taking the umpteenth call of the day, and being asked the same questions over and over. To make matters worse, the publicity material sent out from head office was less than clear about the scope of work they could help with; this often meant he found himself repeating the same sentence twenty times a day, 'Sorry, we can't help.'

Then there were the callers who insisted on talking. Talking non-stop. Petros often considered putting them through to Sylvester. It would be an interesting social experiment: what happens when you put a caller with verbal diarrhoea though to someone who loved the sound of his own voice? Would the conversation go on forever? Would one of them give up, concede defeat to another more skilled in overuse of the tongue? Would one of them ever have to stop talking so they could go to the toilet, or did it only happen that people who didn't talk as much as the other person found themselves in the awkward position of not being able to get a word in edgeways to excuse themselves so they could use the toilet? Did people who talked too much never go to the toilet? Did they stop talking when they were on the toilet? The questions were endless.

The people who talked too much on the phone were the most difficult to deal with. Petros often found it impossible to make himself heard and was regularly forced to listen to customers babbling on for ages. He couldn't cut them off: that would be rude, against company policy. When they finally stopped for a brief moment and he stated, 'Sorry, we can't help,' they invariably felt rejected. 'But I've told you everything... What do you mean?' they would say, dejection in their tone. He would have to repeat, 'Sorry, we can't help.'

The thing that really bothered Petros most, though, wasn't Sylvester or the non-stop phone calls as much as the whole nine-to-five routine. Having to go to work at a certain time, clock-watching, clocking in and clocking out, feeling like a robot.

A few weeks before Petros made his life-changing decision, a friend posted a picture on Facebook with the words: "Who wants to give up on society and go live in a treehouse with me?" This had started something in Petros's brain. A chain reaction. He knew he wanted to get away.

Last summer, Petros had been thinking about his dead-end job while on his annual two weeks holiday, and while he was inwardly weighing up the pros and cons of leaving it all behind, the tour guide called out, 'Can I have everyone's attention, please?'

They'd arrived at an area where large rocks of differing shapes and sizes stood on a piece of land on the banks of a lake. The rocks were strewn haphazardly, but there was enough of a basic round pattern to their cluster to make Petros wonder whether they had some kind of mystical significance. Were they placed there deliberately in ancient times? Was it a miniature Stonehenge, an ancient burial ground, or some other monument?

'These stones are thought to have been constructed about one thousand years ago,' explained the tour guide. 'No one is really sure of their significance, but theories range from them being an old form of sun dial, to an old burial site.'

Petros's eye settled on a cavernous opening in the mountain beyond the lake. He began to wonder whether it had once been someone's home.

'Beyond the large stones, there's a cave,' said the tour guide, as if reading Petros's mind. 'You can't see the entrance very well from here, but if you were to paddle over in a boat, you would see, just above the water level there's a cave entrance.'

Petros's mind became enraptured by the dark entrance and he felt a yearning to get closer to it. He looked around at the mountains and open land, not a living soul for miles around, and wished he could live somewhere like this.

'Our ancestors, of course, used to live in caves,' continued the tour guide. 'This one is quite deep and it's believed to have housed up to fifty people at one time. That could be one of the reasons why these rocks are here. There are theories about a community who used to bury their dead here. In truth, no one really knows whether these rocks are a burial ground. They will probably remain a mystery.'

'Do you think people could live in that cave now?' asked Petros, catching himself unawares as his mind worked overtime. He sensed a curious connection to this place.

The tour guide appeared flustered at actually having been asked a question; the first one of the day. Judging by his reaction, Petros gathered he wasn't used to answering questions, *Or maybe he prefers to babble on uninterrupted like Sylvester.* Petros rolled his eyes at the thought.

With raised eyebrows, the tour guide replied, 'Um... It seems unlikely. With rising water levels the entrance will eventually be flooded. I'd imagine this whole area will be submerged under water in the not too distant future. It's a pity all this history will be gone.'

Petros frowned as he observed the cave entrance, feeling disappointed, as if a dream had been dashed.

∽✵∾

Petros attempted to book the same tour a few months later. He'd hardly been able to stop thinking about the beautiful lake and the rugged mountains and rocks. It had been so tranquil there, and he hadn't been able to recapture the feeling since.

He couldn't find the tour listed on the travel website he'd previously used, so he called them and asked whether he could book it over the phone.

'Sorry, sir, that tour isn't available anymore. It's been stopped on Health and Safety grounds, I'm afraid. It's too hazardous.'

Health and Safety? Petros frowned. After getting off the phone he did a Google search using the name of the area he'd visited and found out the tour company he'd travelled with had been sued for damages following an accident. One of the tourists took a small boat over the lake to access the old cave, having been told by a tour guide that it was habitable. The man had almost drowned in the waterlogged cave.

Petros shook his head as he read the article. He still felt an odd attachment to the place that had bewitched him with its beauty, and dearly wanted to return.

A kind of gloom fell over Petros when he discovered that the tour company no longer travelled to the historical site. He'd felt such an affinity to the place, almost as if it was calling him home. He put it down to his need to escape from his current existence.

The daily grind at the office with the petulant comments made by his co-workers, in particular Sylvester, made Petros question what he had done wrong to end up in such a negative environment. His whole philosophy about life seemed to have changed since returning from the ancient site. It made him more dissatisfied with his mundane day-to-day existence.

The ancients who built the monument lived with some kind of purpose. Their legacy fascinated tourists to the area even now, hundreds of years later. No one would be visiting this call centre in a hundred years' time to take photos of what he and his colleagues were doing. Petros felt a need to be more, *do* more. At the same time, he no longer wanted to be part of this mechanical society. A longing for freedom burned within him and he couldn't help thinking that a window had been opened when he'd visited the old ruins the year before.

So when Sylvester told him the news about a bank manager being found out for fraud and Petros said, 'I never heard about that', and Sylvester replied, 'Where've you been? Under a rock?' Petros knew what he had to do.

Petros felt much happier now. Gone were the days of nine-to-five, alarm clocks, telephones ringing, ignorant colleagues, dreary days of nothing to look forward to. Here he had everything he needed. A sense of adventure filled his every waking moment, and he learned something new each day. He felt a sense of awe and wonder at what nature could teach someone, and what survival instincts could do to create innovation and new ways of living.

Life here, out in the open, was pleasant and deeply satisfying in a way that his office job could never be. He laughed when he thought of the tour company ending their tours here because of "Health and Safety". He had never been more healthy. As for safety, yes, it could be dangerous if you were not careful, but the element of excitement at learning new ways to survive was thrilling.

Petros finally felt fulfilled. The lack of human contact didn't bother him at all. Occasionally, stray deer or other animals would visit, but mostly it was only him. On his own. No one to impose demands. He wasn't sure how long he would stay, but for now it suited him fine.

He'd come to the conclusion that the cluster of rocks might well be some sort of ancient time-keeping method, because the sun cast shadows at different times of day. If he wanted to, he could easily tell what time it was, but Petros was happier not knowing.

The Great Flood

Jade had grown up in the town of Ashedge and had always heard stories about the great flood that had wiped away half of the once bustling seaside town. When she was a little girl, she'd asked her grandmother, on a trip to the beach, why there was a house in the sea and who lived there.

Risha, her grandmother, had replied with tear-filled eyes, 'That was the home of Mrs Better. She was a widow who lived alone. I was about eight when the great flood stole her away. Her name always suited her because if you ever had a problem she could make it better. I once fell over and scraped my knee as a girl; she took me into her house and washed away the pain. She stuck a bright pink plaster on my wound. I was so proud of that. Pink was my favourite colour at the time.'

As she lay sunbathing on the beach, Jade stared at the remains of the old house that was now nothing but a shell. Her two children were building a sandcastle with her husband, Kirk, close by.

Jade's mind always drifted back to the past whenever she visited Ashedge. This was her first visit in nearly three years. Her children had wanted to go to the beach as it was a sunny day, and her husband had suggested coming here. He wanted to see the town she'd grown up in as she talked about it a lot and he'd never visited.

Before heading for the beach, they'd been on a bit of a tour of the town, visiting her old school, and a couple of her parents' friends who still lived in Ashedge.

Kirk left the children next to the sandcastle and walked over to where Jade was reclining on a sun lounger. He sat on a beach towel next to her. 'Lovely beach,' he said, wiping sand off his hands onto the towel.

'Yes, I'd forgotten how peaceful it is here,' said Jade.

'It's beautiful. I think I'll take some photos later. Those old buildings in the sea are fascinating. There must have been a whole town here once that was wiped off the map in a flood centuries ago.'

'The Great Flood,' said Jade, sitting up and facing him. 'It was less than a century ago. My nan told me about it. She knew the old woman who lived in that house.' Jade pointed to the ruins of a little house in the sea. It was nothing more than a nondescript rectangular building now, with large window-shaped holes. 'Mrs Better. My nan talked fondly of her. Her house always had an open door and the local children would visit her and she'd give them treats like homemade cakes, sweets, that sort of thing. She was in her eighties when the flood came and half the town was washed away. Nan said that most people had heard the warnings and evacuated, but Mrs Better's house was the one closest to the sea and she didn't have a chance to escape.'

'How sad.' Kirk frowned and looked out to sea. 'It just goes to show that there's always a story behind everything. That's really captured my imagination. I think I'll hire a boat and go out to the house, take some pictures of the inside as well.'

Later that day, Kirk took their eldest daughter, Risha (named after Jade's grandmother), with him on a boat and they visited the ruins of the house that had once belonged to Mrs Better.

Jade suffered from seasickness so she didn't go with them. She stayed on the beach with their three-year-old daughter, Elisa. They watched from the shore.

After an hour or so, Kirk and Risha returned to the beach.

'Did you have a nice time, Rish?' asked Jade, cuddling her daughter.

'Yes, Mummy.'

'She loved it,' said Kirk packing away his camera into the beach bag next to Jade's sun lounger. 'I even let her take a couple of photos, didn't I, sweetie?'

Risha giggled. 'I took lots of photos.'

'She certainly got a bit carried away,' said Kirk, laughing. 'I thought I'd lost her at one point. I was worried she'd gone into the water, but she was playing hide and seek in the old house.' He turned to look in the direction of the ruined building, squinting as if trying to see it more clearly. 'It's amazing how much room there is in there. Looks so small from the outside. A bit like the TARDIS.' He laughed.

'Mummy, can we go back again?' asked Risha. 'I want to show you the house.'

'Mummy will see the photos, Rish,' said Jade, smiling brightly at the little girl.

'C'mon,' said Kirk, looking at his watch, 'time to pack up and leave. We've got a long drive back home.'

The family bundled into their car. Jade leaned over Risha to fasten the belt on her carseat. She noticed a bright pink plaster on her knee.

'Rish, where did you get that plaster?'

'I scraped my knee in the old house that me and Daddy went to. Mrs Better gave it to me.' The child grinned proudly as she stroked the plaster. 'It's pink like my dress.'

'Kirk!' said Jade, her voice coming out in more of a squeal. 'Y- you didn't tell me Risha fell over when you were in that old house.'

Kirk looked over his shoulder from his position in the driver's seat. 'She didn't.' His brow creased into a frown.

'Well, why has she got a plaster on her knee? Was there anyone else in there?' Jade touched the pink plaster and looked accusingly at Kirk.

'There was no one in there... Maybe she overheard you talking about Mrs Better earlier on the beach.'

'That still doesn't explain where she got this plaster. We don't have bright pink plasters at home.'

'From school, maybe,' suggested Kirk shrugging. He turned back around to face the windscreen.

'She didn't have a plaster on her knee this morning,' said Jade.

'I told you, Mummy, it was Mrs Better. She put the plaster on my knee.' Risha grinned and rubbed her hand over the plaster.

Kirk turned around to look at Jade, who was now looking at Risha, wide-eyed.

Glimmer Siluridae

Shelly and her husband, Frank, were on a weekend break away from home. He'd wanted to do some fishing and she'd wanted a few days where she could relax without constant interruptions from her children or work commitments. Shelly's parents had agreed to look after their five-year-old twins, Sophie and Eric, for the weekend.

Frank's godfather owned a canal boat that he rented out in the summer months. He offered to let Frank and Shelly stay there.

On the Saturday morning, Frank set out early on his fishing trip. He was meeting up with his best friend, Pete. 'See you later, Shell,' he'd called out into the cabin before leaving.

Shelly, still half asleep, mumbled a lazy good-bye.

She woke up about an hour later and, after breakfast, decided to take a walk along the banks of the canal.

About ten minutes into her walk, she saw a bench and wandered over to it, taking the opportunity to rest her legs and absorb the beautiful surroundings. It was the first time in ages that she'd been this close to nature. Her life was spent mostly in buildings or on the busy built-up streets of London: noise, crowds, hardly any privacy, that seemed to be her lot. This trip felt like the perfect way to revive her dwindling spirits.

A young girl strolled along the side of the canal and caught Shelly's eye. Noticing how close to the edge of the canal the girl was, Shelly almost felt obliged to yell at her to be careful. She stood up and approached the young girl. 'Hello,' said Shelly.

The girl looked at her and Shelly noticed the colour of her hair, a deep purple with a silvery sheen; her eyes were the same colour, or was that a trick of the light? Shelly blinked but the girl's eyes remained a mystifying shade of purple. *Contact lenses*, thought Shelly, musing at how fashions had changed since she was a girl. The clothes the girl wore, a sleeveless top and long billowing skirt, were also purple. Intricate embroidery laced throughout the fabric in varying colours, from blues to yellows and reds, seemed to shimmer and change colour as the light caught it when she moved. 'Hello, Shelly,' said the girl.

'How did you know my name?' Shelly put a hand to her forehead and squinted against the sun so she could see the girl more clearly. The sun shone brightly, so much so that there appeared to be a halo around the stranger.

'For once, I'd love it if someone actually remembered me,' said the girl, arms folded, a glum expression on her face. Then she dropped her arms to her sides and smiled brightly.

'Remembered you?' said Shelly, knitting her brow. 'Do I know you?'

The girl waved an arm in front of her to dismiss the question. 'Ignore me, Shelly,' she said. 'All will become clear soon enough. I suppose it's just hard being at the gateway all the time.'

'The gateway?'

'Nothing to concern yourself about.'

'Um... I was just going to say I think you're walking a bit too close to the edge of the canal,' said Shelly. 'It's dangerous. They really should have railings here, or a sign or something.'

'Oh, don't worry. I'm happier it's like this. Makes it easier.'

'Easier?'

'Yes, for the passing.'

'I don't understand.'

The girl smiled and said. 'If I'm being honest, I quite like this part because you won't remember anything I say.'

Shelly frowned and began to wonder whether the girl had perhaps taken hallucinogenic drugs of some kind; she did look a bit like a hippie.

'By the way, I should introduce myself. I'm Glimmer Siluridae. I'm here to take you home.'

'Home?' Shelly blinked, then said, 'Did Frank send you? Is that how you knew my name?'

Glimmer shook her head.

'Why would we be going home?'

'Because it's time.'

'Frank and I are supposed to be here for another day.'

'I should probably explain. But no, that'll happen tomorrow. For now, all you need to know is, I'm a mermaid and I'm taking you home. Tomorrow at six o'clock in the evening, you'll be here again. There'll be a sprinkling of stars on the surface of the canal and they will contain a spell that will compel you to return to your kingdom. At that time, you will also be ready to return. It probably sounds like gobbledygook to you now, but rest assured everything is as it should be. Your husband and children will grieve but it's a part of their life lessons on this plane. You'll all be reunited when their journey is at an end.'

Shelly stared blankly, slightly concerned for the girl's mental health.

Glimmer twirled around on the spot and Shelly noticed that the surface of the canal was sparkling. She looked at Glimmer, and then back at the water, and noticed star-like twinkles on the canal as it reflected the sun. Glimmer waved at Shelly and, after taking a few steps back, she danced forward on her tiptoes and dived into the water.

Shelly gasped. Almost instantly, the surface of the canal returned to normal, leaving no trace of the purple-haired girl. Shelly stood staring at the water for a few moments in a daze. She was left wondering whether any of it had actually happened. *Did a girl really just tell me she was a mermaid and then disappear into the canal?* Her concern for the girl reared its head and she began to walk away quickly to try to find some help. Something her daughter, Sophie, had once said flashed through her mind: *'Mummy, I used to be a mermaid. Before I was born.'*

I've been spending too long reading children's stories, thought Shelly as she made her way back to the boat. With each step, her memory of meeting the young girl faded more and more, so that by the time she'd returned to the canal boat she'd completely forgotten about Glimmer.

☙

Frank returned to the boat in the late morning after having caught a few fish for their lunch. They enjoyed a relaxing afternoon on the boat.

Shelly wished they could remain there for a while longer, sad that they'd have to return home to the routine of city life so soon.

'We can always take a trip here more often,' said Frank as they relaxed on the sofa in the evening. 'We can bring the kids the next time, too; they'd love it here.'

'They would,' said Shelly. 'But the canal should really have railings; I was thinking that earlier when I went for a walk. There was a young girl... too close to the edge. She could have fallen in.' In Shelly's mind she remembered a young girl with purple hair and hippie-like clothing strolling along the edge of the canal, but had no recollection of their conversation.

'There *are* railings,' said Frank.

They went outside, Shelly insisting there were none. To her surprise, there were indeed railings at the water's edge. 'I must've been mistaken,' she said, her mind feeling foggy.

☙

The next afternoon, Frank and Shelly went for a walk along the canal.

'It's so peaceful here,' said Frank. 'Makes me want to leave the city.'

'Me too,' said Shelly.

After they'd been out for a while, he looked at his watch. 'It's nearly six o'clock, already. We'd better get back to the boat and start packing.'

'Hmm... So depressing,' said Shelly, screwing up her face.

They walked along hand in hand and soon came across the bench that Shelly had been sitting on the day before. 'See? Here there are no railings, and that's where the girl was,' said Shelly. Then she spotted some wildflowers growing by the bank. 'I'm just going to pick a few of these flowers; Sophie would love them, yellow's her favourite colour.' She let go of her husband's hand.

'Be careful, honey, I don't want you falling in so I have to rescue you. This suit's expensive. You'll have to pay for the dry cleaning.'

'Ha, ha.' Shelly approached the canal and noticed stars forming on the surface.

'Shelly!' Frank cried out.

A few seconds later, she'd disappeared under the water.

಄಄

'Shelly!' Frank could not swim. Trembling, he fished his mobile phone from his pocket but found there was no signal. He ran to the boat where his phone could pick up a signal to make a call. Frantically, he dialled 999.

Within minutes, an ambulance arrived and a rescue team began to scour the canal for Shelly. There was no sign of her.

಄಄

Shelly saw the stars forming on the surface of the river and took a deep breath before jumping in.

Once under the water, she opened her eyes and recognised the girl who had been on the bank of the canal the day before.

'Hello again, Shelly,' said Glimmer, her purple hair looking even more silvery and sleek now they were in the underwater environment.

Shelly could hardly believe that any of it was real. How could she be breathing and seeing everything so clearly under water?

Hesitating for a moment before opening her mouth to speak, still unsure if this was a dream, Shelly asked, 'What's happening? Am I a mermaid now?'

'No,' said the girl with a swish of her fishtail.

Shelly took in the blue and purple scales that glittered so beautifully as the girl moved. Then Shelly looked down, expecting to see her own legs, but instead saw a shimmering red and yellow tail. She caught her breath and slowly looked up at the young girl. 'Y-you said I'm not a mermaid.'

Glimmer giggled and it sounded like a song: a song Shelly knew but could not place in her memory.

119

'You asked me if you're a mermaid *now*,' said the girl. 'That's why I said no. You're not a mermaid "now". You've always been a mermaid.'

Shelly swished her tail and something in her mind recalled a world long forgotten but still there at the periphery of her consciousness.

'Please come with me and I'll show you where you need to be,' said Glimmer.

'I probably should be getting back,' said Shelly, 'my husband will be wondering where I am.'

'Death is not the end, you know. Your soul is on a journey and your human time is done. Follow me to the world where you belong.'

As Shelly followed, she became aware of the graceful movement of her tail and it felt natural, like swimming this way was something she'd always done. Her memory began to become hazy and thoughts of her husband and children drifted far away as she remembered the friends and family she was to be reunited with.

'The family has missed you, Lunaria,' said Glimmer.

'I've missed them too.' Shelly answered to the name *Lunaria* without a second thought.

'Welcome home,' said Glimmer, flicking her tail as they arrived at the underwater cave.

'It feels so good to be back.'

Lost In You

Standing at the edge of the pier tonight, he knew it would feel like this. Something about the unknown depth of any body of water fascinated him, and lately he'd been feeling a pull, almost a yearning to just lose himself in the deep. To disappear.

He'd never learnt to swim. When he was growing up, many tried to teach him but failed. At primary school he'd been given swimming lessons. Everyone else in his class passed the swimming tasks and got their badges, were able to say they could swim. He couldn't seem to grasp the skills required to move in the water, an innate fear of drowning most probably the reason. Funny how all these years later, it'd turned into a kind of awe. He now looked at rivers, seas, lakes, oceans, with the eyes of someone who'd fallen in love and wanted to be lost in the hold of his beloved.

For the past few months he'd ignored these strange feelings, keeping clear of expanses of water of any kind, fearing the power it seemed to have over him.

Tonight Ralph had allowed himself to approach the edge of the pier. He knew it would feel like this.

The first time he'd felt the "pull" had been when he'd moved away from the city and bought his home overlooking the marina. He'd been mesmerised by the view of the sea when he first visited the house with the estate agent and had inwardly mused at how an element of danger was always important to make something truly beautiful.

Tamsin had crossed his mind at the same time as that thought. Beautiful Tamsin, who'd broken his heart. It wasn't unusual, though; Tamsin was always on his mind.

When he'd first seen her across the bar of a pub at a boring office Christmas party, over twenty years before, he knew then, in an instant, that she would be the love of his life. He'd just come out of a bitter relationship. Kirsty left him for his best friend Terry a few months earlier. Good old reliable Terry. Funny how you could know someone for years but never really know them.

The moment he saw Tamsin, he felt as if he'd known her for a hundred years. She'd smiled at him and he knew immediately that she could break his heart with a mere flutter of her eyelashes. It didn't stop him from approaching her and asking if she would like a drink. They became inseparable; they were inseparable for years.

Now, over twenty years since their first meeting, the times they'd spent together seemed almost imagined. Ralph had fled the city soon after Tamsin left him, unable to face the barrage of memories it held. Twenty years was a long time to be in a relationship with someone, and it'd ended so suddenly. He could still sometimes feel her presence at night. It felt like more of a comfort than a fear.

He'd convinced himself that when she left she'd taken some of him with her; after all, every time someone touches something, a bit of their DNA is left behind, isn't it? Over the years, he felt sure they'd become one. The couple had a habit of holding hands when walking along the street together, and they never spent a night apart. They were forever touching each other, holding each other. It made him happier to believe that some part of her would be with him always—her DNA must have mingled with his so now they were each another part of the other. Even death could not change that.

When Tamsin left that night, he'd followed, not ready to accept that their relationship was ending.

'I've met someone,' she'd explained, staring at the door as she spoke, as if eager to escape and begin her new life.

'You can't leave... Not now... Not like this...'

She took hold of her suitcase handle and wheeled the case towards the front door, oblivious to his plea. 'Sorry. Maybe it's just that we've been together for so long. It's become so... I don't know... *Routine.*' A shrug as she cast a brief, apologetic glance at him from under heavy eyelids. 'Sorry,' she repeated after opening the front door and making her way outside.

'Don't leave me,' he cried out to the back of the front door, behind which she had disappeared.

Looking in at him from the side of the door, she said, 'I do still love you, Ralph. I'll always love you, I'm just not in love with you, not anymore.'

Words he could not accept.

So he'd followed her, and he'd begged her to spend one last evening with him, celebrating their past before letting it all go.

His memories of that evening were so precious to him, he kept a tight hold on them. They'd revisited the restaurant where they'd had their first date, and then they'd strolled along the banks of the Thames, where the lights had glistened making the bridges look magical.

'Look at the lights, Tammy, it's got to be some kind of omen. We were meant to be together. Please stay.' He'd kissed her but she'd pulled away.

'It's over, Ralph. I'm sorry.'

His mind became hazy from there. All he could remember was shouting something at her, and there'd been an almighty splash. She'd fallen into the river. Once in the water she'd struggled. That was one of the many things they'd had in common: Tamsin couldn't swim either.

She'd screamed for help, but he'd walked quickly away. *It's for the best,* he thought. *If she's not mine anymore, no one else should have her.*

It was only when he heard a familiar ring tone—the sound of her mobile phone—that he remembered he was carrying her handbag and suitcase. He stopped walking and took her phone from the bag. It had stopped ringing by now but there was a text message from someone called James: **Where are u?** It stated, **I'm waiting.**

Her lover. The thought made him feel sick. He replied to the message: **I've left Ralph, but I need time alone. I need time to think. I will contact you when I'm ready. Don't try to call.**

The perfect crime; the words entered Ralph's mind before he had time to digest what was happening. He pressed "send" on the phone and then threw it into the Thames.

Getting rid of the suitcase and handbag would be harder. He looked down at the small case and wondered what he could do with it. He could not throw it into the river, it was likely to float on the top, or be seen. Scratching his head, he wheeled the suitcase along behind him and turned towards the main road. There was a large commercial waste bin at the side of the road and as he approached it he saw recycling containers beside it. One of the containers had a picture of shoes on it, the other had clothes, the other was for paper, and there was also a bin for glass.

Ralph emptied the contents of the suitcase into the various containers. She'd only packed a few pieces of clothing and shoes. Sweat formed on his brow as he realised what he was doing. It was as if he'd planned to kill her and get rid of the evidence. Tears welled in his eyes as he began to regret not helping her. He hated himself, would give anything to see her again.

Unable to think straight, he dumped the suitcase into the commercial waste bin and reached for her handbag. He could not help looking inside the bag. Her purse sat at the top. He lifted it out and on opening it saw her driving licence: her photograph. Placing the licence in his pocket, he discarded the rest of the handbag and contents into the large bin and walked away.

That night, he stared at the photograph on the driving licence for hours. It was the last of her possessions that he owned. When he'd looked in the wardrobe and drawers in their bedroom on returning home that evening, he found that she'd already removed the rest of her belongings. She must have been planning her exit for months.

When friends asked about Tamsin, he said she'd left him, packed her bags, told him she'd found someone new. His friends sympathised with him.

The city became unbearable. It was the place they'd spent so many years planning for a future that could never be. Within days, he put the flat up for sale and began to look for a new place to live.

&

When Ralph first saw the house by the marina, with the view of the pier and the boats in the harbour, he felt a sense of freedom.

In some ways, he felt closer to Tamsin here, away from the city. Rivers and seas were connected, after all, weren't they? Sometimes he imagined her calling out to him from the sea, calling him to join her.

&

Standing at the edge of the pier tonight, he knew it would feel like this. He knew he'd feel closer than ever to Tamsin. It would take just one brave step and then he could join her. They'd be reunited in the deep, mysterious, endless ocean. No one could separate them ever again.

Kneeling down, he turned around, pulling himself off the edge of the pier. 'I love you, Tammy,' he whispered as the water claimed him. He disappeared beneath the calm surface and didn't struggle. After a brief swirl of ripples, the sea became still once again.

The Memory Remains

For Cilla, birthdays always evoked nostalgia and made her more aware of the passing of time. Memories that had been filed away would surface and she'd find herself remembering people and events from years gone by. Sometimes the memories were sweet, sometimes bitter, but there was no escaping her habit of thinking of the past and reminiscing.

They were expecting about fifty people at the party. Many of those invited were old friends and Cilla hadn't seen most of them for years. Just the thought of meeting up again with people she'd known in her twenties, who'd now be in their forties, made her feel quite old. Catching sight of her reflection as she walked past the mirror in the hallway, she wondered whether her wrinkles were too prominent. *Maybe I should have used night cream,* she mused. It struck her that time was ruthless, and quite obsessive; it refused to hold back the aging process for anyone. With a frown, she turned away from the mirror. She didn't resent growing older, as such, but was always conscious on birthdays how time persisted in slipping away, slowly, gradually, almost inconspicuously. In Cilla's opinion, as well as suffering from Obsessive Compulsive Disorder, time was also a sly devil, doing everything underhandedly.

Cilla was single. Her last relationship had been over four years ago with a man who didn't want children. She'd left him for that reason, as she'd wanted to start a family. He now had a child; after their relationship broke down, he'd married a twenty-something girl and Cilla had reassured herself at the time that it must have been "on the rebound", but they were still together and she often saw them with their son in the local park.

Now forty-one, Cilla was beginning to accept she may never have children of her own. Time, she surmised, was also quite cruel, and the more she pondered it, she felt sure time must be a man. It was *Father Time*, after all, she mused. Although it couldn't all be blamed on gender, as *Mother Nature* also played *her* part in the conspiracy.

Knowing that Gus was coming to the party, Cilla couldn't help feeling nervous as she approached the kitchen. Her sister, Hollie, had asked if she could come early to help out with the preparations for the barbecue. It was Hollie's husband's birthday. A big birthday. His fortieth.

Twenty years before, they'd been part of a gang of friends that included Hollie's boyfriend (now husband) Leo, and Gus. They'd been a close-knit bunch with the same interests, same sense of humour. Carefree students.

Cilla fell in love with Gus slowly but surely, and they'd ended up having a bit of a fling. None of the "gang" were aware they'd been in a relationship, they just thought they were good friends. He'd left her for another girl and she'd been devastated. During the summer break from university, he told her he was going to see his parents for a couple of weeks. Next thing she knew, he'd settled in his old hometown with another girl. She discovered his betrayal on overhearing a conversation between Leo and her sister: 'Oh, Gus has moved back to Bristol, shacked up with some Aussie girl who came over to study here,' Leo had said. 'Really? It's about time he found someone, I suppose,' was Hollie's response.

That short time they'd spent together as boyfriend and girlfriend left a giant footprint in Cilla's heart and she'd never forgotten him. Today her nerves were jangling at the thought of seeing him again, even though she knew time had changed everything and he was married now.

Cilla had been approaching thirty when she heard that Gus was getting married. After a couple of bad relationships, she'd been looking back sentimentally, and Gus's name came up in conversation. She found out he'd invited Hollie to his wedding.

It wasn't unexpected that he'd invite her sister and neglect to invite her: Hollie had always been closer to him (apart from when Cilla and Gus were dating) because her husband and Gus were best friends at university. It didn't stop Cilla from crying for three consecutive days after she heard about his impending marriage, though; whenever she was alone, floods of tears had flowed relentlessly.

'Hey, Cilla!' said Leo, greeting her as she walked into the kitchen.

'Hi Leo, Happy Birthday,' said Cilla, handing him a plastic bag containing her gift and a card.

'Thanks. Here, let me introduce you to Estelle, Gus's wife. You've never met, have you?'

'Er... No,' said Cilla, turning her attention to the blonde woman who stood by the cooker stirring something in a pan.

Estelle looked at her and grinned. 'Lovely to meet you. You must be Hollie's sister?'

'Yes.'

When she reached out a hand, Cilla noticed her nails were perfectly manicured with a glittering nail polish. She hadn't had time to paint her own nails before coming. Estelle's wedding ring was the next thing that caught her eye; it graced her ring-finger next to a wonderfully large diamond engagement ring.

Cilla shook her hand, trying to ignore the precious gem. *That could have been mine*. The thought took her by surprise as memories of her brief relationship with Gus flashed into focus. They'd talked about the future a couple of times. He'd once said, 'I don't think I'm the marrying type, but if I was I'd marry you.'

Youth. A time when the whole world lay ahead and anything seemed possible. She'd laughed at him and responded with: 'I'd have to agree to marry you first.' She did wonder, the next day, if her reply may have given him the impression that she didn't love him. Over the years, as time trod its steadfast path, those words played back in her mind, tainted with regret.

'We're making dessert at the moment,' said Estelle brightly.

Cilla felt quite plain in comparison to this woman whose hair was sleeked into a fashionable shoulder-length style and who wore a dress that clung to her perfect shapely figure. She'd obviously made an effort to dress up. Cilla wondered how she managed to walk in her heels, which appeared to be at least five inches high.

Cilla was wearing jeans and a top with a few sequins on it. Dangly earrings were the one thing she'd really put on in an attempt to dress up. Only visiting her sister's house, she hadn't felt a need to wear anything special. She wished she had now.

Hollie, who'd been in the garden, walked into the kitchen after Leo went outside. 'I see you've met Estelle, Cilla.'

'Yes.'

'Gus is outside helping with the barbecue. I think we'll leave the boys to it. You know what men are like.' She giggled, as did Estelle.

Cilla felt compelled to join in so faked a laugh, but it came out a bit too late and the others looked at her as if they'd missed a joke. She smiled and shrugged, cringing slightly.

'How's everything going?' Hollie asked Estelle.

'Almost done. Only the strawberries to do now.'

'Okay, great. It was kind of you to bring those. Did you say you grow them?'

'Yes, in our back yard. Gus is addicted to strawberries. I wasn't so keen but he showed me a way to eat them that I absolutely love! We melt chocolate—I've got some in the pan over there—and dip the strawberries in it. Always goes down well at parties, and it's so quick to prepare.'

'What a coincidence!' said Hollie. 'Cilla, you love strawberries dipped in chocolate too, don't you? That's usually her speciality at parties.' Hollie giggled.

'Ooh... Well, you can help prepare them then, Cilla, That would be fab,' said Estelle.

Cilla watched as Estelle went over to the cooker and picked up the pan of chocolate. Her mind went back to a night from the past.

It had been Gus's birthday and they were expecting a few of his friends for dinner. Cilla had been helping to make a strawberry cheesecake for dessert, but the mixture became curdled and looked—and tasted—horrible.

'I'm not giving that to my friends.' He screwed up his nose. 'I thought you said you knew how to make cheesecake.'

'I do. It must be the cheese. It's not the usual kind of soft cheese that I buy.'

'We should have just bought a dessert. What are we gonna give them now? I suppose we still have the strawberries that you bought.'

'I've got an idea!' she said.

'What?'

'Do you have any chocolate?'

'Er... does a bear shit in the woods? There's plenty in the cupboard over there. You know I'm addicted to the stuff.'

Cilla melted the various chocolate bars and they used the mixture as a sauce for the strawberries.

Gus was so impressed that he'd called them "Cilla's Chocberry Delights" when serving them to friends and told her he would never have thought of it himself and that she'd "saved the day".

'Here you go,' said Estelle, placing the pan on the table.

Cilla's mind snapped back to the present.

'I'll let you do those as you're an expert.' Estelle chuckled. 'I'm going to check on my son. He's only seven. I'm worried Gus'll have him helping out with the barbecue. Men have no brains.' She snorted.

Gus walked into the kitchen shortly after Estelle had gone outside. His eyes met Cilla's while she was in the midst of dipping the strawberries into the chocolate sauce. He smiled at her and seemed to stare for the briefest moment.

His appearance was different enough so that she could separate him in her mind from the man who'd been her first love. She remembered the long wavy hair he'd had in his youth. He'd shaved his head, or perhaps gone bald, she couldn't tell which.

'Hello. Cilla, isn't it?' he said eventually, acting almost as if they'd never even met.

'Er... yes. Hi, Gus,' she said, trying to sound like she had her life together and wasn't still pining after dreams of yore.

He glanced at the chocolate-covered strawberries, which she'd placed on a ceramic plate in a circular pattern.

Gus turned his attention to Hollie, who was preparing a salad. 'Do

128

you have another skewer by any chance, Holl?'

'Yes, over there.'

'Thanks.'

He took the skewer and left the room, taking with him the last fragments of Cilla's bygone fantasies.

She didn't speak to him again that day; they just exchanged a few awkward smiles. They were now strangers. Time had seen to that.

The Chocolate Fiend

'It's always a chocolate handprint.' The inspector rubbed a hand over his bearded chin in thought.

'Is it the killer's hand? What about fingerprints?' asked Detective Pebbles enthusiastically.

'No. He uses the victims' hands and makes a handprint on the wall of their bedroom.'

'Bedroom?' The detective scratched his head.

'Well, so far he's killed three women, all aged between twenty-five and thirty, and all in their bedrooms.'

'Is there a sexual motive? Rape?'

'No. No sexual assaults as far as we can tell. He just slits their necks —one clean slice—and uses their hands to make the handprints.'

'Wow, that's weird,' said the detective.

'It is. I can honestly say that in my thirty years in the job I haven't come across something quite as eerie and gruesome. He has some kind of obsession with chocolate. May be a psychological link there.'

'Hard to see how chocolate could motivate someone to kill.'

The inspector nodded. 'He calls himself "The Chocolate Fiend". Leaves a calling card.' He handed a business card sized piece of cardboard to the detective.

'Handmade. Can't we trace this to a source?'

'We are trying, but it's a fairly common piece of cardboard and the printing could have been done on any PC.'

The detective handed the card back to the older man. 'Is this being linked to any other murders?'

'Only the two other chocolate-themed ones. There haven't been any similar murders in recent years.'

'Are there any DNA results we can use to check for a criminal record? Any fabrics found at the scene, fingerprints, hair, etc.?'

'He has been very careful. Probably wears gloves and some other kind of protective clothing,' said the inspector, a faraway look in his eyes.

'You keep saying "he", Inspector. Are we sure it's a man?'

'All factors would indicate that, but nothing can ever be guessed with real certainty. All lines of enquiry are being followed.'

The two policemen watched as the victim was carried away in a body bag.

DC Pebbles winced at the sight of the handprint on the wall. 'Inspector, do you think the handprint was made when the victim was still alive? Otherwise, how did he—the killer, manage to drag a dead body over to the wall without covering the place with blood, and how would he have placed the body back on the bed so neatly?'

Inspector Rose turned to his colleague. 'Unless there's more than one killer. But no, it seems more than likely it's only one man, a psychopath with an ego problem.' He held up the calling card and rolled his eyes. 'I do wonder, however, if he knew his victims and somehow convinced them to make the chocolate handprints before killing them.' A stern frown on his face, he left the room.

৩৯৵

Josh clicked the name on Rosanna's profile on the online dating website. The description made him smile: **I like horses, cats, and I'm addicted to chocolate!**

This is gonna be too easy, he thought to himself.

He sent her a message and, as she was online, Rosanna replied immediately.

They agreed to chat and swapped telephone numbers.

He phoned her straight away. 'I really love your profile,' he said, smirking. 'You are so pretty and we have so much in common. I like horses and cats, too.'

'Oh, that's great.'

'Would you like to meet tomorrow? I'll bring chocolate,' he said.

'Mmm... How can I resist.' Rosanna giggled.

৩৯৵

Robert knocked on the door of the flat. The tenth floor of a high rise in South London. He'd been given the address by a friend.

Suzie opened the door. 'Hi, you must be Robert.'

'Yes.'

'How much do you want for it?' she asked, eyeing the plastic bag in his hand.

'A hundred.'

Her eyes widened. 'Wow. Um... Okay. Thanks. I'll er... get the money.'

She closed the door behind her and returned a couple of minutes later.

He took the cash, and while he counted it, she took the plastic bag and hesitantly peeked inside.

131

'Nice doing business with you,' he said.

'Yeah, uh, thanks.'

Suzie felt her hands shaking. She'd never done anything like this before. Placing the plastic bag on the coffee table, she caught her breath. Her immediate thought was: *Oh my, God! What have I done?* Images of handcuffs and police cells raced through her mind. Robert might tell someone, accidentally reveal her identity... or even *deliberately*; after all, she didn't know anything about him.

Grabbing the plastic bag, Suzie ran into her bedroom and placed it under the mattress, all the while trying to shake off the anxiety. She recalled what her contact had said about Robert, describing him as an ex-criminal who now tried to stay out of trouble, for the most part; he made his living selling illegal firearms. But she didn't really know the person who'd introduced Robert... couldn't even remember his name; she'd met him in a pub that a friend of a friend had told her about. How could she trust any of them?

She'd never used a gun before, wasn't intending to use this one but felt she needed it for protection. If she had to use it, she would. Sixty years old and she'd never so much as received a parking fine, and here she was contemplating murder.

Josh met Rosanna at *Pizza Express*. Her choice. He went along with it as it was a cheap option, even though he hated pizza. Tonight there was one thing on his mind. Everything else faded into insignificance. After tonight, he'd move on to the next victim. He grinned to himself at the thought.

They began to eat their pizza in relative silence, an awkward smile here and there.

'S-so you like horses?' asked Rosanna.

'Yeah, and cats.' He couldn't help grinning as he said it, revealing green herbs between his teeth and stringy cheese at the corner of his mouth. 'Coincidence, or what?' He winked at her.

She smiled.

Shortly, Rosanna excused herself to go to the toilet and he found himself almost regretting what he was planning to do to her. She was sexy: shapely with a trim figure, bright blue eyes; there was a real innocence about her. He shook away the sentimental thoughts. He'd promised himself never again would he fall for a woman, not after Zena. She had stolen his heart and torn it to pieces. He'd loved her more than life itself, but she'd been using him, had never loved him. Her last words to him were: "I wouldn't love you if you were the last man on earth!"

Zena had been cheating on him for months. He'd planned their future together but ended up lost and alone. It took him a year to even think about dating other women and when he finally did, he realised how much fun it could be to take control. He used them, just like he'd been used. Pretended to love them but caused them pain. It was a way to get back at Zena and women like her.

৶৽৶

Aaron stood by the cooker, melting chocolate on the hob. He then filled two Thermos flasks with the sticky liquid. Storing them in his bag, he made his way out of the kitchen.

His mother stood in the hallway. 'Off out?' she asked.

'What's it got to do with you?' he said gruffly.

'Um... I'm your mother.'

'Yeah, some mother.'

'What's that supposed to mean?'

'We live in a fucking run-down housing association flat and I'm supposed to be grateful?'

'Aaron!' she practically screamed the word. 'Show some respect! How could you? I've done the best I can for you since your dad left us.'

'Oh, who cares?' He pushed past her towards the front door.

'You're twenty years old, Aaron. You should be contributing, working... instead—'

He twisted around to face her. 'How? I can't find a fucking job. I'm an ex-criminal. No one wants me.'

'It was an accident. You served your time,' soothed his mother.

'Huh! I probably did you a favour killing Henry. One less mouth to feed.'

Her eyes welled with tears. 'Stop blaming yourself. It was an accident... you didn't mean—'

'No, of course I didn't fucking mean to kill him. If I did, I wouldn't have got caught.' He stormed out of the front door.

A flashback took hold and he remembered accidentally reversing his car over his brother, who'd been sitting next to the garage door listening to music on his mp3 player. Henry had been a child: thirteen years old. Aaron was seventeen at the time; he'd only recently passed his

133

driving test. He didn't even know he'd run his brother over and only noticed something odd in the rearview mirror as he drove off the driveway. At first, he'd thought it was an injured dog as Henry lay curled up, wearing all black clothing.

He'd held his breath and got out of the car and then recognised his brother on the ground, one arm raised, his hand jammed up against the garage door. He'd been eating a chocolate bar, but the chocolate had spread over his palm and stuck his hand to the garage door.

Aaron reached to pull it away, leaving a smeared chocolate handprint. He hadn't allowed his mother to wash it off for weeks.

His mother suffered a breakdown while he was in a Young Offender Institution. She lost her job, lost the house they'd been living in. By the time he was released, she'd moved to this housing association flat; their new home.

✹

After their evening out at the pizza restaurant, Josh and Rosanna sat on the sofa in her living room.

'I don't usually bring men back here, you know,' she said, blushing. 'Not on a first date.'

'That's okay, I won't try anything,' he lied through a grin.

'Would you like a drink?' she asked, standing up.

'Yeah, wine—if you've got some.'

'Um... I was thinking more like tea or coffee.'

'Don't worry, I won't try to get you drunk.'

She smiled and blushed again as she turned towards the kitchen. A few moments later she returned with a bottle of white wine.

'I feel I can trust you,' she said whilst filling two wine glasses. 'It's so hard, these days, to find someone you can trust, isn't it?'

'Yes, it is.'

'Online dating is so risky. I'm sure there are so many players out there.'

'I'm sure there are,' he said, lifting up his glass. 'Cheers!'

'Cheers,' she echoed.

'I'm looking for serious commitment,' he said, eyes fixed on his wine glass. When he looked back at Rosanna, he saw that her face had brightened and he felt the slight twinge of remorse for what he was going to do; he shook it away.

'Me too! See? I knew I could trust you,' she gushed.

'I really like you,' he said to his wine glass.

'I know it sounds weird, but I feel a connection between us, you

134

know, like we've known each other for ages,' she said.

'Oh, definitely, I feel it too. Felt it straight away. As soon as I read your profile and saw you like horses and cats, it was like we must have known each other in a previous life, or something.'

Rosanna giggled. 'Yeah, like maybe we were owners of race horses and had a few cats.'

'Yeah, and we liked eating chocolate.'

Rosanna laughed. 'Yeah! We would've been fat!'

'Ha, ha! Speak for yourself.'

The evening continued in a similar vein until the couple finished off two bottles of wine and ended up in bed together.

'Uh... Wow! I wasn't meaning for this to happen,' said Rosanna as Josh took off his pants and climbed under the sheets.

'Me neither.'

'You said you'd brought chocolate?' she said. 'Was that the bag you were carrying this evening?'

'Oh yeah. I forgot about that.' He leapt out of bed and ran into the living room to retrieve the plastic bag.

Returning to the bedroom, he opened the bag and took out two bars of chocolate. It had been quite a warm evening and they'd melted slightly.

'I have an idea,' said Rosanna, unwrapping a sticky bar of chocolate. She began to spread the melted chocolate on her breasts. 'Would you like to try it?' she smiled provocatively.

'How can I resist?'

For the next couple of hours the couple used up the confectionary bars, inventing new ways to enjoy chocolate.

Josh woke up at 5 a.m. and took a quick shower to get rid of the remaining chocolate and then sneaked out of the flat, feeling a little sad. He really liked Rosanna and they'd had fun. Once again he pushed away the thoughts and took out his mobile phone.

He sent her a text message: **Had fun but I don't think it'll work out between us. Was nice while it lasted X**

He planned to check out the dating website later and find another willing partner. He was back in control and it felt good. He couldn't help but smile as he walked away.

Rosanna woke up to the sound of an alert from her mobile phone letting her know that she had received a text message. She sat up and in the half-darkness saw the shape of a chocolate handprint on the sheet; a reminder of the night she'd spent with Josh. A frown forced away the smile that was developing. Usually it didn't bother her, loving and leaving these desperate online-dating types, but Josh seemed so nice. It would probably break his heart if she ended their relationship so soon. She rolled her eyes, knowing it had to be done. The last thing she wanted was a serious relationship; she'd been there and done that, and bore the emotional scars to prove it.

She picked up her mobile phone, ready to send him a text, the usual 'It's not you, it's me... blah, blah, blah...' Then she saw the text from Josh. She sighed, expecting a lovey-dovey message thanking her for last night. Her mouth fell open as she read it: a little part of her heart died. He'd dumped her. It hadn't happened before. She was always the one to end it. A tear came to her eye as memories of their night together filled her mind.

'Huh!' she said aloud, shaking away the morose thoughts and swiping her unshed tear. 'You've saved me the trouble, Josh.'

She stood up and changed the sheets, half-smiling, half-frowning at the chocolate stains that remained.

৩৯৻

Suzie heard Aaron return home, slamming the front door. She looked at the alarm clock beside her bed. The red numbers showed 4:13 a.m. Letting out a sigh, she went back to sleep.

Aaron went into the bathroom and took a quick shower. He watched the blood trickle down the plughole, the remains of tonight's victim.

This one had been awake. Usually he caught them unawares while they slept, pouring chocolate on their hands, making them leave a handprint on the wall while he held a gun to their head. They were invariably hysterical, so he made sure he tied a cloth around their mouth to muffle any screams before they woke. With this one, he'd had to struggle, but on seeing the gun she'd clammed up and remained silent. Probably in the hope he'd let her live.

The most important thing for Aaron was getting the handprint right. He needed to make the prints, to remind him of Henry so it would be something they did together. He did it all in Henry's memory. Aaron always took photos of the handprints using his old Polaroid camera. He was running out of film for that and it wasn't cheap. But it was the best way to take the photos without leaving a trace of them elsewhere.

He kept the photos under his bed at home. He liked to look at

136

them.

$\wp\!\!\sim\!\!\infty$

The early-morning news told the story of another young woman, Sheila Reynolds, who'd been found with her throat slit, a chocolate handprint on the wall, the calling card left by the killer. The fourth victim of The Chocolate Fiend as far as police knew.

Suzie stared across the kitchen table at her son.

'Aaron, have you heard about these murders?' Her voice broke slightly.

'A fucking weirdo. But he's good though. Never gets caught.' Aaron stood up and finished off the last piece of his toast.

'Did you do this?' asked Suzie, pointing at the television.

'Do what?' Aaron shrugged. 'I'm going to the job centre.'

'Did you kill these women?' Suzie stood up, red-faced, and took something from the pocket of her apron. A photo. A Polariod photo. She held it up.

'You bitch! What were you doin' in my room?' He grabbed her hand and snatched the photo. 'I'm gonna kill you!'

She caught her breath. 'Like you killed those women? W-what's wrong with you? I'm calling the police!'

Aaron grabbed a knife from the cutlery drawer and held it in front of him. 'Call the police and I'll fucking kill you.'

Suzie took her mobile from the kitchen table. Hands shaking, she began to dial.

Aaron lunged towards her.

She stepped back and pulled the gun out from the drawer under the table where she'd hidden it. Pointing the weapon at her son, her hand unsteady, eyes streaming with tears, Suzie said, 'Don't make me do this, Aaron.'

'You ain't got the guts,' he jeered. Aaron approached her waving the knife in front of him. 'I'll kill you with this knife before you even work out where the fucking trigger is.'

Suzie shook violently as he moved closer, her nerves getting the better of her. She pulled the trigger without even knowing she'd done it. The noise resonated through the flat.

Aaron fell to the floor. The bullet had pierced straight through his eye.

The Great Painter

Julie spun around quickly, realising too late that someone was standing directly behind her in the queue waiting to be served. Her cup of hot chocolate flew out of her hand and onto the floor, creating a large puddle that looked a bit like a chocolate-coloured inkblot test.

Mouth wide open, Julie raised her eyes from the spilt drink and came face to face with the man who'd been standing behind her.

'Sorry,' they both said at once.

'No, it's my fault,' said the man, waving a hand to dismiss her apology. 'I was standing too close, wasn't looking, too busy with my phone.' He rolled his eyes to suggest he felt embarrassed. 'Let me buy you another, uh—' He squinted at the mess on the floor, 'Hot chocolate, was it?'

'Um... I—' Julie watched as a member of the café staff arrived with a mop and set about cleaning the floor.

'Don't worry,' said Julie to the man, 'I'd better get to work.' She felt flustered and not in the mood to talk to this stranger. He was very handsome, but that made her feel sad for some reason, so she had to hold back tears.

The young man shrugged and turned around to order his drink.

Julie hesitated slightly, kicking herself for letting the moment slip by. This man might be a godsend, someone to take her mind off the past and everything that had gone wrong. Louis had left her six months ago and she'd spent most of those months feeling lonely but not wanting to talk to anyone. She'd found herself constantly making up excuses as to why she couldn't go out with friends; that behaviour had driven most of them away.

Her self-esteem had sunk to an all-time low. She wanted to tap this young man on the shoulder, and say 'Actually, I will have that hot chocolate', but how desperate would that seem? Julie reluctantly walked away towards the door.

'Wait!'

It was the man's voice. She turned to face him.

'Here you go,' he said. 'I asked the barista to make it just the same way for you.'

He had a contagious smile.

It had been a long time since she'd really smiled.

'I'm going to sit over there. Would you like to join me?' he asked, pointing to a couple of bar stools next to the window.

Julie didn't really have to go to work. She'd been sacked from her job quite soon after Louis left her. They'd been married for ten years, were childhood sweethearts. One day, quite unexpectedly, he told her that he'd met someone else. His new girlfriend was much younger than her. Louis announced that he wanted a divorce because his mistress had become pregnant and he "wanted to do the right thing".

'Really? Really?' she'd exclaimed. 'It's doing the "right thing" to have an affair, is it? What planet do you live on?'

'You're just bitter, Julie!' he retorted, snarling. 'You can't have kids and now you're jealous.'

Speechless, Julie watched him leave and wondered if she'd ever really known him.

She hardly slept for weeks afterwards as she tried to make sense of it all. She'd arrive late for work, always trying to find a good reason, but she worked for a large corporation: they had no loyalty towards staff. If she couldn't get to work on time they'd find someone who could.

When she lost her job, she stayed at home, locked herself away for months, only venturing out of the house to sign on at the job centre. She'd not yet been able to secure any job interviews. Everything seemed to be spiralling downwards.

'Um... I can probably spare half an hour or so,' she said to the kind young man.

'Great! I'm Rupert,' he said, reaching out to shake her hand.

'Um... Julie,' she said. His hand felt warm and she held onto it a bit longer than necessary as they shook hands.

They sat in awkward silence for a minute or two. He sipped his coffee and she stared at the hot chocolate he'd bought her, wondering what to say.

'Er... thank you for buying me this drink,' she finally said.

'Not at all. It was my fault. And anyway, it's nice to meet you.'

His expression was warm and sincere. She noticed his blue eyes and became lost in them for a moment. 'Nice to meet you too,' she said, blushing when she realised she'd been staring at him. She felt silly getting ideas about this man. He appeared to be in his twenties, whereas she'd soon be forty.

'I believe in fate, you know, things happening for a reason,' said Rupert. 'I think we were meant to meet.'

'Or I was being clumsy,' said Julie, a joke to cover up her nerves.

'No. I was staring at my phone. I have officially become part of the zombie generation who stare at their phones, oblivious to the world around them. I always swore I'd never turn into one of them.'

Julie giggled. 'I don't own a smartphone for precisely that reason. I don't want to get obsessed with it.'

'It's easy to get carried away on these things,' he said, twirling his phone around in his hand as he spoke. 'But if I hadn't been staring at it, I'd never have met you.'

That smile again, and she couldn't help smiling back.

They chatted for a while and Julie ended up telling him all about her failed marriage. Somehow it was easy to talk to him; maybe because he was so far removed from the situation. He revealed that he'd also recently come out of a long-term relationship.

They agreed to meet again that evening for a drink at the local pub.

As they exited the café, Rupert glanced at her and then looked around him.

'It's lovely weather today,' commented Julie.

'The Great Painter at work,' he said in reply.

She frowned and he noticed her confusion.

Grinning, he said, 'I believe there is something bigger than us: a force that more or less steers our lives in certain directions.'

'Ah, yes, you said you believe in fate.'

'I call it The Great Painter.'

'That's an interesting way to look at it,' said Julie.

'I think The Painter did a wonderful job today, bringing us together with the spilt hot chocolate. That was one of his better masterpieces.' Rupert kissed her on the cheek.

Julie smiled.

'See you tonight.' He waved as he walked away.

Julie made her way home, her mind full of memories of Rupert and dreams of what could be.

Somewhere in Time

The café's name was painted on the glass in flowing red writing, which from the inside read backwards: '*L'horizon*', said Eliza, reading the name. 'Interesting name for a café.'

'The place where the sky appears to meet the sea or land,' said Phillip. 'There's something about the horizon that's misleading.'

'What are you on about?'

'You could travel for hours believing that somehow when you reach the edge that would be the end, but when you get there you just have to keep on going.'

'Um... I think we all know by now that the Earth isn't flat.'

'Yes, the Earth's round, so eventually you'd end up where you started if you keep going in the same direction. Round and round. It's one of life's great lies.'

'I think you need more wine,' said Eliza, taking the half-full bottle of rosé out of the ice bucket and topping up his glass.

'I was thinking about it when I was on the beach today,' he elaborated.

'You think too much,' said Eliza, looking out of the window at the fading light of dusk.

'But isn't that how it works? Nature reflects life. Or maybe we're supposed to get some kind of message from nature.'

Eliza took a sip of wine and listened to the soft music playing in the tiny café. The next day they would be heading back to London and leaving this quaint little town behind.

'You're not listening to me,' said Phillip.

'I am, you're just getting a bit boring.'

Phillip picked up his smart phone and began clicking a few buttons.

'Now who's ignoring who?' said Eliza with a giggle.

'I'm not ignoring you, I'm trying to find that photo I took of you at the beach today. It was so nice having it all to ourselves, wasn't it?'

'Yes, it's a pity we can't stay here forever,' said Eliza

He flipped his phone around to enable her to see the photo. 'You look like you're the last person on Earth there.'

'It was very calming at the beach,' said Eliza. 'Perhaps we could go back for a little while before we leave tomorrow.'

'Okay, it's not far from the airport.'

Eliza glanced around the café. 'It's quiet for eight o'clock in the evening, isn't it? I would have expected more people to be here.'

'I actually prefer that it's just me and you. It makes it more special.'

'Me too, but the food's lovely here, you'd expect it to be full of people.'

'Where's the waiter gone?' asked Phillip. 'We should really pay for our meal and leave. I want to get an early night, we'll be travelling for most of the day tomorrow.'

The old man who'd served them appeared from behind a curtain at the back of the café and walked towards them.

Eliza watched Phillip raise his hand in the usual way someone would to get a waiter's attention, and she almost laughed out loud at the absurdity of the gesture. The man was already walking towards them, and there were no other customers.

'Can we have the bill, please?' asked Phillip.

'Of course. Was everything to your satisfaction?' asked the man.

'Yes, thank you,' said Eliza and Phillip together.

'It was delicious,' added Eliza.

'Yes, perfect,' said Phillip.

The man smiled and walked away.

'It was nice to get away,' said Eliza, reaching across the table and taking Phillip's hand.

'I'll miss this place,' he said. 'It's so different here, hardly any people at all, not like London where we have to practically fight our way through a crowd every time we want to go somewhere.'

'I'd like to retire somewhere like this,' said Eliza.

The old man returned with a piece of paper. He handed it to Phillip and walked away.

Phillip opened his eyes wide when he looked at it.

'Is it *that* expensive?' asked Eliza.

Phillip turned the paper towards her. The handwritten note read: *As you are the last people on Earth, the meal is free.*

Eliza laughed. 'He must have overheard our conversation.'

Phillip laughed with her. 'We have to pay him, though, it was such a nice meal.'

'Why can't you just be thankful for the gift?' said Eliza. 'Follow your advice from earlier and take it as a message from nature; everything's free out in the wild, right?'

Phillip shrugged.

'Look, the man wanted to treat us,' she continued. 'Who are we to argue? Anyway, he's disappeared again, let's just go.'

As they left the café, Phillip turned back to look at the place. 'I feel bad, like we've just stolen something.'

Eliza took his hand and led him away. 'He knew we were on holiday and he wanted us to have a nice experience here. The locals in these sorts of places are always very friendly, not like London, you're just not used to it.'

'You're probably right.'

As they walked along the street, Eliza couldn't help but notice how deserted it seemed. 'Talk about a one-horse town.' A feeling of hollowness surrounded her as she spoke. 'In a way, I'll be glad to get back to London tomorrow; it's quite eerie when there's no one around for miles, isn't it.'

'Oh, I don't know, I think I prefer it,' said Phillip.

They reached the door of the Bed and Breakfast where they were staying. All the lights were out.

Eliza glanced at her watch. Still before 9 p.m., yet no one was around.

'Looks like everyone's gone to bed,' said Phillip as they walked up the stairs.

'We might really be the last people on Earth,' said Eliza, giggling.

Eliza woke the next morning and found herself alone in bed. Stretching, she listened out for any sound from the en suite. Nothing.

She stepped out of bed and approached the bathroom. 'Phillip?'

He wasn't in there.

Maybe he's gone to get breakfast?

She showered and changed into her jeans and a sweater. They'd be travelling later; they'd packed everything yesterday afternoon when they got back from the beach.

Pulling her suitcase towards the door, she looked around and noticed that Phillip's suitcase was nowhere to be seen. Perhaps he'd taken it with him so he'd be ready to go when they finished breakfast. Last night's conversation came to mind: they'd been planning to go back to the beach before heading out to the airport.

Eliza took her mobile phone out of her handbag and tried calling Phillip's number, but it just kept ringing. She sent him a text instead: **Where are you?**

A few minutes passed with no response. Her stomach rumbled, so she decided to go and get breakfast without him.

Something caught her eye as she stood up, a note on the bedside table. Recognising Phillip's handwriting, she smiled and swiped the note. *Why didn't I notice that before?* Her smile faded when she read it: *You're the last person on Earth.* For some reason, a chill ran through her and she felt as spooked as she had when they were walking along the empty street the evening before. She shrugged away her concern and told herself it was obviously Phillip's idea of a joke; he would probably be waiting for her in the breakfast room.

The breakfast buffet had been set up as usual, but there was no one else in the room when Eliza arrived. Looking at the clock on the wall, she saw that it was nearly 9 a.m.; perhaps everyone had eaten and left already. Strangely, though, the buffet appeared untouched. She checked her mobile phone. Still no reply from Phillip. *Maybe he's at the beach.*

She took a plate and chose a few bits of fruit and a croissant then poured herself some coffee, still finding it hard to shake the eerie feeling that had come over her. She ate her breakfast quickly and glugged down her coffee, eager to leave the abandoned place.

Eliza made her way to the beach, pulling her suitcase behind her. Her breath came in short bursts as she felt her anxiety level rise. There was no one around; not in the B&B, not on the streets, not even in the tourist area of the resort. She was feeling quite shaken by the time she arrived at the beach where she'd spent time with Phillip the day before.

He wasn't there.

She let go of her suitcase and walked towards the sea. Sitting down on the stony beach, she remembered she'd sat in the same spot the day before. Something Phillip had said at the restaurant came to her mind: '...the Earth's round, so eventually you'd end up where you started if you keep going in the same direction. Round and round...'

She heard footsteps crunching towards her and turned around to see Phillip.

'I just got a great photo of you sitting there, Eliza!' he said.

'Let's see.' Taking his phone, she glanced at the photo then smiled as she handed the phone back to him.

'It's a shame we have to leave tomorrow, isn't it?' he said.

'Yeah.' She felt sad about it too.

'I saw a little café in town earlier, *L'horizon*. It looks nice. Maybe we should go and pack so we're ready for the trip, and then head to the café for dinner tonight,' suggested Phillip. 'What d'you say?'

'Sounds good,' said Eliza, standing up and hugging him.

Sand and Water

The stars made way for a blue sky, almost cloudless. Audrey had slept fitfully, but mostly she'd been on high alert. Watching, waiting. Was she destined to die here?

Audrey had been lying there for hours, encased in sand. She'd struggled to shake free at first, but that only resulted in her flip-flops being kicked off. Snippets of the conversation between her two assailants replayed in her mind: *'What about covering her head?'*; *'He didn't say kill her, did he?'*

Giggling throughout, those lunatics apparently found it funny to completely bury her up to the neck and then run off. Complete strangers. Two young women, more like teenagers. One of them was called Tracy; Audrey knew that because the other girl—the shorter, plumper one—shouted out as they were leaving: 'Are you sure we should just leave her here, Trace?'

Tracy answered with, 'It's what he paid us to do, ain't it?'

Their laughter and chatter moved further and further away, leaving Audrey in the sand cocoon where she spent the night.

Someone paid them, arranged for them to bring her to this beach and bury her alive. The girls had mentioned *him* a few times: *He said this, he said that*.

Who was "he"?

Throughout her terrifying night alone under the stars, Audrey's mind concocted strange dreams, in between the bursts of alertness when she strained to hear any noise and worried in case anyone found her here in this vulnerable position, yet prayed that someone would. The persistent train of thought nagged her: *who would do this?*

Bradley was the first person she suspected—her work colleague. He had quite a competitive nature, and they were supposed to be meeting an important business client together at the office later today. Bradley may have wanted the glory of being the one to meet the client and report back to their boss. It made her sad to think he'd do something this sinister. He hadn't struck her as the devious type; she'd thought they could be good friends—maybe even more than friends.

They'd been out for a drink together at the local pub the evening before, and she'd hoped it might be the start of something special between them; now she wondered whether the whole thing had been nothing but a ruse.

Audrey first noticed the two girls—her attackers—at the pub.

They'd glanced at her a couple of times and appeared to be gossiping and giggling. Audrey hadn't taken it seriously; she'd assumed they were just young girls making fun of the sequined flip-flops mismatched with her designer skirt-suit. (Temperatures in town had reached record highs that day. The air-conditioning unit in the office broke down. Audrey's pumps felt tight and uncomfortable as a consequence. At lunchtime, she'd gone shopping for sandals but failed to find any in her size. Having only twenty minutes left of her lunch hour, she'd settled for a pair of sparkly flip-flops, hoping they were smart enough for office attire).

Did Bradley know the girls? Had he arranged for them to be at the pub so they could see their victim? She didn't want Bradley to be behind this. She liked Bradley.

He'd left the pub at about 7 p.m. after only one drink. That came as a disappointment to Audrey, as she'd hoped they would be spending more time together, but he explained that he wanted to go home early to prepare for the meeting with the client.

After finishing her drink and going to the toilet, Audrey had headed out of the pub. She'd deliberately taken the route to her house that offered the best view of the beach. Ever since moving to this seaside town, she'd made the most of the scenic walks. This was only a six-month secondment; soon London life would resume, amidst the crowds and pollution.

Audrey felt very hot, and perspiration spilled from her brow. The sun had risen a few hours ago and continued to beat down relentlessly. She felt sure it wouldn't be long before she sustained severe sunburn—her pale skin burned easily: either sunburn or sunstroke, one of those would probably seal her fate. She felt doomed.

She'd been abandoned there in the late evening. The girls had obviously followed her home from the pub because they knew where she lived—or, more likely, *he*'d given them the address, whoever *he* was.

Tracy visited her at home at around 9 p.m., posing as a council worker who wanted feedback on improvements they were proposing to make in the local area. The girl appeared genuine, holding a clipboard and wearing a badge bearing the council's logo. Even though Audrey recognised her from the pub, she hadn't suspected a thing. She'd followed Tracy to the pier because the girl said it would be easier to explain the plans for the pier extension at the local beach if they had a look at it. Audrey's interest was piqued because her office dealt with local property sales and she wanted to get up-to-date information to pass on to her boss in the hope it might lead to a promotion of some kind. It could also be of interest to the important client she'd be seeing the next day, a way to impress him.

Audrey only started to suspect something wasn't quite right when Tracy asked her to wait on the beach while she went back to her car to retrieve the plans. Sunset had come and gone by then. Not sure how she'd be able to see any of the plans in the fading light, Audrey considered saying 'Perhaps we should wait until tomorrow', but Tracy fled before she had the chance.

The next thing she knew, a blanket fell on Audrey's head and she was pushed to the ground. All sorts of thoughts ran through her mind. She cursed herself for following Tracy. How many times had there been warnings on TV and social media about new methods being used to lure and trap women? She froze in horror as she imagined being held captive and all sorts of terrible things happening to her. Would she be killed? All the time, she blamed herself; *you stupid fool, so gullible, idiot.*

She'd heard mainly giggling from the two girls, along with a few words here and there as they manhandled and buried her: *'You grab her legs,'; 'How much did he say he'd pay us?'; 'We should have got the money up front'.* At one point, one of them said: 'I don't really like this,' and Audrey dared to believe that they would let her go, that they'd grown tired of her pleas, screams, and tears. Her hope faded when the other responded: 'We've got to do it, or he'll kill us.'

Audrey racked her brain trying to work out who *he* might be. Her ex-boyfriend, Leon, came to mind. They'd split up not long ago, and he had known she would be moving to this office for six months. The impending secondment played a big part in their break-up; he accused her of loving her career more than she loved him. Leon wasn't really the vengeful type, but what if the way they'd parted had left him with unresolved anger resulting in this cruel reprisal?

Not knowing who'd paid these girls to do this was almost as bad as being stuck here. If only one of the girls had mentioned his name. Maybe they did say it but she'd missed it when screaming loudly for them to let her go.

By Audrey's reckoning, she'd been trapped here, buried on this beach for at least ten hours, if not more.

With the sand packed so tightly, she could feel the vibration of her pulse.

Thankfully, the tide couldn't reach this far, so there hadn't been any risk of drowning. Whoever hated her didn't want her dead. A small consolation. Perhaps, though, he wanted worse for her; not a clean and quick drowning but a slow death brought on by hunger and pain, and fear. She shook those dark thoughts away.

147

If she'd been closer to the sea, she mused, it may have been easier to shake free. The water might have washed over the sand little by little, loosening it from her body. Those girls obviously knew what they were doing; they didn't want her to escape. Would they come back? Would "he" show his face?

For some reason she thought of news stories where people walking their dogs found dead bodies. *What if I die here? No one would find me for days.* She imagined her rotting flesh being eaten by vultures. Were there even any vultures in the UK? Perhaps they'd make the journey especially to eat her. She shook the nonsensical thoughts and images from her mind.

Audrey had lived in this area for a couple of months and knew this part of the beach quite well. Every Sunday she came here with a book and a latte, to lose herself in fiction for a few hours. She'd found it to be the perfect tranquil setting to de-stress after a long week at work. It was such a beautiful place that she often wondered why no one else ever seemed to set foot here. Was there some secret about it that she didn't know? Maybe it didn't exist at all and she was in some other dimension; that would explain why no one had heard her screams and why she never saw a soul here. Maybe she'd dreamt it, maybe she was dreaming now. She almost laughed at the crazy theories running through her mind. Besides, it wasn't strictly true that no one came here. There was one man, an old man she'd once seen here: Gerard.

Gerard had introduced himself and told her he used to live in the area as a boy, that he'd often played on this part of the beach with his younger sister. He'd called it a "special place". Up until today, she'd considered it one of *her* special places. Now it had become her nightmare.

'Whenever I come here, I remember playing with Lucy,' said Gerard. 'This used to be our special place. My little sister would run into the sea knowing that I'd have to run in to get her. Our parents always looked to me as her guardian when we were playing together. I was a couple of years older.'

'It's lovely that you have such memories,' said Audrey. In reality, she'd been hoping the old man would go away as she'd reached a particularly interesting chapter of the novel she was reading.

'Lucy was my best friend for many years. I don't think I ever got over her death.'

'Sorry to hear that,' said Audrey, looking back at her book.

'There'll always be a part of Lucy here. This is where I come to remember her.'

Audrey frowned at him.

He stared out to sea for a while. 'It's been nearly fifty years.' He peered down at her. 'Well, I'll let you finish your book in peace.' Walking away he tipped his top hat towards her.

Audrey watched him go, feeling slightly guilty for not showing interest in his story. It was obviously important to him. He was probably a lonely old man who needed company. She pondered how old fashioned he looked in his suit and top hat; he struck her as being lost in the past. After thinking for a moment about what he'd said, she shook her head and got back to her novel.

Audrey found herself praying Gerard would return today. He did say he came here often to remember his sister. *Please let him come here today*, she found herself thinking.

As if by magic, the next thing she heard was Gerard's voice. 'We meet again.'

Relief washed over her. 'Thank God,' she said.

'I'll make a bargain with you,' began the old man.

'What?' She frowned in frustration. It seemed an odd thing for him to say and didn't make sense.

'I'll help you out if you promise me something,' he said.

She squinted up at the man, who stood there in a full suit and top hat in all this heat. 'Look!' she huffed, a bit too aggressively. 'Sorry.' She sighed. 'I'm not really in the mood for jokes. I'm tired. Can you help me? Two girls buried me here; I have no idea why, and I can't get out. I've been here all night.'

'I know,' he replied.

She blinked and looked up at him.

'I asked them to,' he added.

'Excuse me?' she blurted, but then regretted the forceful manner, realising that she still needed his help. 'Um, look, I don't know who you are or what you want, but—'

'Oh, don't play the innocent with me!' he boomed. 'You know this is my land. You have no right to be here, but each week I see you sitting on the beach acting as if you own the place. Let me tell you, this place was mine and Lucy's long ago; long before you were even born. This is my land, and you don't belong here.'

Lost for words, Audrey opened her mouth but then closed it again. This man was obviously delusional or mad, or both.

'I'll set you free if you promise never to return.'

'I—I—' A multitude of thoughts ran around Audrey's mind. Who was he to decide where she could or couldn't go? What would the police make of this? This wasn't his land, it was a public place. In the end, with no alternative option, she bit her tongue and said, 'Okay. No problem. I think I've had enough of the place, anyway.'

The old man revealed a plastic shovel that he'd been holding behind his back. He dug her out of the sand in complete silence.

She wobbled as she stood up, her legs quite numb from being

trapped in the sand overnight.

Gerard tipped his hat towards her.

She retrieved her flip-flops and turned to leave.

'She's gone now Lucy, she'll never bother us again,' she heard him say as she walked away.

Thank you for reading.

If you enjoyed this collection of stories, please consider telling someone else about it, or leaving a review on Amazon or other online bookstores.

More books by Maria Savva:

Short story collections:

Pieces of a Rainbow
Love and Loyalty (and Other Stories)
Fusion
Delusion and Dreams
3
Far Away In Time
Lost and Found

Novels:

Coincidences
Second Chances
A Time To Tell
The Dream
Haunted
The Spider
Evil Never Dies (The Spider - Book 2)

Other short stories by Maria Savva can be found in the BestsellerBound anthologies.

About the author:

Maria Savva lives and works in London. She is a lawyer and academic tutor, specialising in Family Law. Her day job involves providing Clinical Legal Education to Bar students and trainee solicitors. She has been writing fiction for over 25 years. Her novels and stories are often inspired by real life. Find out more at http://www.mariasavva.com